ROSE
1854

PRAIRIE ROSES
COLLECTION
BOOK 18

RENA GROOT

I pray my writing honors and glorifies God.

This book is a work of fiction. Any references to historical events, real people, or real places are used fictitiously.

© 2022 by Rena Groot
All rights reserved

First Edition April 28, 2022
ASIN: B09SHPJ5Q2 (eBook)
Print ISBN: 9798417538698

Available in Print, eBook, and (eventually maybe) Audiobook

Sneak Peek of Aria
©2022 Shonda Czeschin Fischer

Cover art by Randi Gammons of Randi Gammons Graphic Design
Branding for series by Chatona Having

Editing and Formatting by Fixer Fairy, Lia McGunigle & Debbey Cozzone

Table of Contents

Dedication 5

Chapter One 7

Chapter Two 17

Chapter Three 29

Chapter Four 41

Chapter Five 51

Chapter Six 61

Chapter Seven 71

Chapter Eight 79

Chapter Nine 89

Chapter Ten 97

Chapter Eleven 105

Chapter Twelve 113

Chapter Thirteen 119

Chapter Fourteen 131

Chapter Fifteen 137

Chapter Sixteen 142

Chapter Seventeen 147

Chapter Eighteen 157

Epilogue 167

Sneak peek of Aria..170
All the 2022 Prairie Roses Collection Stories:.....177
Acknowledgements...183
Author's Note...183
All of Rena's Titles..185
About the Author..193

Dedication

*I fully realize everything we have
is a gift from God.
We can do nothing and we have nothing
apart from Him.
I am thankful He gave me a love
(okay, an addiction) for writing.
I dedicate this book to God for His glory.*

*I also dedicate Rose to my newfound
brother and sister,
Tara and Travis Taylor.
I am so thankful I found you.*

Chapter One

April 1, 1854

Rose plunked herself down on top of her steamer trunk and sobbed. Her heart surely must be broken, it hurt so badly. How was it possible she'd been denied passage on a wagon on the Oregon Trail?

"Naw, there ain't no room for a single woman on this here wagon train." Captain Whittaker punctuated his sentence with a chunk of raw tobacco spit towards her feet. The shock of his words and actions left her speechless. She'd even offered to pay double the fare, but he appeared immovable. Being determined to help him understand how badly she needed to get to Oregon didn't change his mind at all.

Why hadn't anyone told her that rule—an unaccompanied woman would not be welcome on a wagon train? She sold almost everything she owned, except for the contents of the steamer trunk and the clothes on her back, left her teaching position at an all-girls school, and had given up the last room at the only woman's boarding house in town. She cried into her silk hanky as the desperation of her situation hit home.

Now what, Lord? Do you not want me in Oregon? Did I misunderstand Your direction? Would the hardships of the trail prove to be too much for me? Maybe the sacrifices would be too great? You know all things, God. Do I lack the strength and courage for the trail? Are you closing the door? God, help!

She felt like she was invisible as people bustled about her loading their wagons for the trip. She suddenly smelled a strong whiff of new leather.

Where did that come from?

Through her brimming tears, it surprised her to see a pair of cowboy boots firmly planted on the ground in front of her, close to the hem of her skirt. She looked up to see who they belonged to and was astonished to see a pair of the kindest eyes she had ever seen.

"Howdy, ma'am. I couldn't help but overhear your talk with the captain…"

Rose surveyed the man, as much as propriety would allow. He looked to be in his early twenties, tall and blonde. His blue eyes spoke of honesty and sincerity. His clothes were simple but clean. He held the reins of a beautiful stallion in one hand while squishing his hat in the other. He grinned…

"The name's Lachlan, ma'am. Lachlan James Smith. When I heard how the captain spoke to you, I prayed for you, and about your troubles. I asked God to make a way for you to join this train."

Lachlan paused and looked like he found words difficult to speak. His eyes suddenly looked determined. As he cleared his throat, he said, "I have a proposal you might be interested in. I believe it's an idea God gave me. I would never have come up with it on my own."

Rose dabbed at the tears on her face trying unsuccessfully to gain her composure.

A proposal? What is this man talking about? Is he meaning marriage?

"My name's Rose Caroline Murphy. I'm sorry, Mr. Smith, because of this predicament, I couldn't help but cry."

"I understand, ma'am. I imagine it'd be pretty upsetting."

"Please, call me Miss Murphy."

"Ma'am, I mean Miss Murphy. I don't rightly know how to ask this…"

What could this man possibly have to say that could help me?

"I'm heading out with Captain Nelson T. Whittaker for Oregon. I'll be mighty busy with caring for the animals and pulling guard duty. I'd greatly appreciate a cook, someone to help me."

"I'm sorry...what are you saying?" Lachlan looked so uncomfortable Rose felt sorry for him. His hat brim suffered much abuse in his big hand.

"Ma'am, I mean Miss Murphy, if you agree, I could sign you up as part of my wagon contents. Oh, that sounds terrible. Sorry. I mean, you would be my traveling companion. I had thoughts I might starve to death, and wondered how I would manage." He smiled sheepishly.

Seeing the horrified look on Rose's face, Lachlan quickly explained. "I mean, if this would work for you, I'd be glad to chaperone you and see you safely to wherever you're going. I'd sleep under the wagon at night. The wagon would be yours. It would all be very proper."

Rose breathed a sigh of relief. She hadn't been exactly sure what he might propose, but she sure didn't want to be part of anything scandalous. Was the man really offering to give up his bed and sleep on the hard ground for her?

"Would Captain Whittaker approve of me going along with you, Mr. Smith? After all, I'm not your wife."

"Please call me Lachlan. It makes me feel ancient to be called Mr. Smith. Well, I planned to ask him right after you said how you felt about the idea. I would pay your passage as a thank you for cooking my meals and taking care of my wagon."

Rose thought for a moment. She really had no other options. He would pay her fare? How very generous of him! The use of the wagon alone cost him about four hundred dollars. To pay for her fare would be another five hundred dollars on top of that.

"I accept your proposal, Mr. Smith. I would love to be your cook." She noted the relieved look in the man's eyes. "It's very kind of you to offer, but I think I should pay my own way."

"No, if you're coming along to help me, I insist on paying." Lachlan smiled. Rose noticed how his face lit up when he smiled. "I'll speak to Captain Whittaker."

"I'll go with you. He just told me I couldn't travel on his train. I'd love to see his face when he hears I have a chaperone."

"Well, your circumstances just changed, ma'am. I mean, Miss Murphy."

As they approached him, Nelson T. Whittaker had a look on his face that said, "Not you again!"

What he did say was, "I ain't changin' my mind. No unaccompanied women are allowed on this here wagon train!"

About to spit tobacco at Rose's feet again, the man nearly choked on the wad when she smiled sweetly before saying, "But I'm no longer unaccompanied, sir."

Captain Whittaker's face turned red, obviously not a man to be trifled with. Lachlan seemed to notice the man's frustration so he quickly spoke up. "I have offered to be her chaperone."

The captain's face clearly registered shock as Lachlan continued. "I have offered to see the lady safely to her destination."

"What do you propose for sleeping accommodations? I'll have no tom foolery under my watch."

"Of course, sir. I have offered to sleep under the wagon."

"Well then, miss, it looks like you'll be part of this here wagon train after all. There better not be any trouble."

Rose opened her purse to pay, but Lachlan stepped in front of her. "I've hired her as my cook, sir. Here's her passage money." He dropped a few gold nuggets into the boss's hand, more than enough, she supposed. Standing to the side, she couldn't help but notice the joyful look on her new hero's face. He seemed so thankful God provided him a cook. She'd definitely been blessed! And by such a handsome gentleman!

As they walked away from the very perplexed looking trail boss, Lachlan asked, "May I carry your trunk to our wagon, ma'am? I mean, Miss Murphy."

"Thank you. I'm surprised Captain Whittaker agreed."

"Why wouldn't he? You have a chaperone, and he has a handful of gold."

Rose felt some irritation at being treated like a child.

Land sakes! This is 1854. Why do women need a chaperone? I can take care of myself.

Smiling sweetly as Lachlan picked up her steamer trunk, she noticed he made it look as if the heavy trunk carried only feathers.

He might be shocked to know what it held.

After placing the trunk in the wagon, Lachlan glanced at Rose. "Do you have any special grocery items you'd like me to pick up?"

That's when Rose realized how unprepared she was for a six-month journey across the continent. What had she been thinking? She possessed no list; no groceries either. This man must think she was a bit daft.

"I threw my list away, but I can get the list from my brother." *Maybe I should have told Lachlan I can't cook—*
"Let me know if there's anything special you need."
Am I being deceitful? He has to know the truth.
"Mr. Smith..."
"Ma'am?"
"Would you still want me along as your cook if I told you I can't cook?"
"You can't cook?"
"No."
He grinned at her. "Well, you can learn. Can't be that hard."
Relief washed over her. "I can make tea."
"That's a great start."
"I'm sorry. I should have said something sooner—before you paid for me."
"It's fine. My sister-in-law, Willow, will be traveling on this train. She's a great cook. She'll help you."
"Thank you."

That night Rose slept in a covered wagon for the first time. She awoke in the blackness of early morning unsure of her whereabouts. Used to silk sheets and eider down quilts, it seemed strange waking to a crunchy cotton coverlet and the sound of canvas flapping.

It took a few moments to get her bearings, then she grinned. She was really in a wagon being outfitted to head out on the Oregon Trail. A dream come true! Too excited to sleep, she went over the miraculous details of the previous day.

Leaving the boarding house had been surprisingly painful. She lived there for her first two years of teaching, right after training at the teacher's college. The matronly Mrs. Morgan, owner of the house, was like a mother to all five girls. She took her duty seriously to educate them in all manner of etiquette. Rose learned so much from this gentle, caring woman. Mrs. Morgan asked the girls to call her Ma. Rose would never admit this to anyone, but she loved Ma more than her adopted Ma.

The girls were like sisters. They cried as she hugged them goodbye. So many tears. The chances of seeing them again in this life were slim. They all knew they were saying goodbye until eternity.

Then there was Thomas G. Taylor. She had no trouble saying goodbye to this man of wealth and prestige, a man who pinned his hopes on having her for his wife.

Nothing but a deep, godly love will ever persuade me to marry. Dear God, please lead me by your Holy Spirit. Help me never to run ahead of you. Please always make Your will clear to me. Thank You, Lord, for hearing my prayer.

She had refused Thomas's marriage proposal.

How could she possibly accept? Life sounded stuffy and boring living in a mansion. She had no desire to be surrounded by doting servants and way too much finery for a person to ever feel comfortable in her own home.

Besides, Rose knew he didn't love her. He wanted a trophy wife, someone to look beautiful in his home, like an exotic piece of furniture.

She could envision her future with that man and it looked grim. He wanted someone who would be submissive to his every wish. Having a mind of her own and an adventurous spirit would definitely not be an asset. Her spirit would have to be quelled, squashed down into a small corner of her being until there would be no Rose left. She'd end up being a hollow, empty, unloved shell.

She had far too much life, passion, mischievousness, and adventure in her to be tempted into a loveless marriage—no matter how advantageous the match seemed to her family and friends. The girls in the boarding house all thought she was crazy and announced they hoped Thomas G. Taylor would notice one of them.

Only Ma seemed to understand Rose's heart. They sat in the boarding house parlor, sipping tea and eating cookies, just the two of them. Rose knew it would be the last visit she would ever have with this dear woman, so she cherished every second.

"Rose, you must follow God, no matter what. It doesn't matter if your parents liked Thomas and thought him someone worthy of you. They don't have to live with him."

She couldn't help but laugh. "My mother took one look at his mansion and liked him instantly. I love my mother, but honestly, I'd rather be in a shack with someone who loves me than a mansion where I am as loved and needed as a chair."

How she loved Ma's laugh. "Rose, you are such a precious woman. I'm sure God has a special man who will love and cherish you. He loves you too much to have you settle for anything less."

"Oh, Ma. You're so kind, but I don't want to meet anyone. I have a dream I want to pursue, and I don't need a man."

Ma just smiled. She said a lot, just the way she smiled. Her eyes said, "Just be patient, my dear Rose, and trust God."

Hugging her precious Ma goodbye left them both crying.

"Please write me and tell me how things have fared with you."

Rose had a passing moment of grief as she thought about her adoptive mother. Mrs. Murphy asked her NOT to write. Mrs. Murphy cut loose the apron strings because Rose wasn't following her wishes by marrying a wealthy socialite. When she said goodbye to Rose, it was forever.

"Naturally, I'll write. I'll miss you, Ma Morgan."

"I love you, Rose. I'll miss you. God be with you and protect you."

As Rose lay in the wagon, listening to the sounds of the night, she began to ask questions.

Did I really sense God's leading? There are so many teachers in Independence—many without work. I heard there are empty school houses in Oregon because there are no teachers. Ever since I heard that, I knew I had to be there. They deserve the opportunity to learn. I'm determined to give some of them that chance.

She remembered Ma's last words. "Now dear, be careful on the trail. There are so many dangers. Watch out for snakes in the grass and snakes among men."

Her mind came around again to Lachlan James Smith. He wasn't a snake. She didn't have to be wary of him. How she thanked God for that man rescuing her from an uncertain future.

He paid my passage? Five hundred dollars? Are cook's wages that high? That's quite the salary. Oh wait! I don't believe I thanked him. He must think me terribly rude.

Her mind rested on the kindness she saw in his face that spoke of nobility and integrity. Just then she heard loud snoring coming from under the wagon.

Oh, this could be a long six months…

The new day finally dawned. As she jumped out of the back of the wagon, she was surprised to see Lachlan busy preparing coffee and cornmeal mush.

"Mr. Smith, I thought that was my job."

"It's okay. We aren't traveling yet, and I was up early."

"I didn't thank you for paying my fare."

Lachlan smiled. "My pleasure, ma'am."

She noted again how his face lit up when he smiled.

"I'll take you to meet my brother and his wife after breakfast. Willow's from the Sioux nation. They are expecting their first child in about four months. I'm sure she'll be grateful for your company."

After the tin dishes were cleaned up and stored in the larder on the side of the wagon, Lachlan led Rose down the line of wagons.

"Owen and Willow, this is Rose Murphy, my new cook."

Both faces registered surprise. Owen reached out a paw of a hand that enclosed Rose's. "Happy to meet you, ma'am."

Rose smiled at them, but Willow just stared at the ground.

Is she shy?

"I'm happy to meet you both."

The woman briefly glanced up at Rose, flashed a brief smile, then quickly looked down again. Rose noted the roundness of Willow's belly. She looked closer to delivering a baby than four months from now. Rose determined then and there she was going to be good friends with this woman.

"Owen, I threw away my supply list. May I borrow your list so Rose can see if she needs anything? further"

"Of course. I'll fetch it."

Rose stood smiling at the beautiful Indian woman, and wondered how she could become her friend. Did she even speak English? Well, she could try…

"Willow, Mr. Smith hired me as his cook, but unfortunately, I don't know how to cook. Will you teach me?"

Her black eyes looked up for a moment, then down again, but the twinkle said yes. Rose smiled.

"Here it is, Lachlan. Supplies are getting low. Best go as soon as possible."

Rose surveyed the list. "That's a lot of supplies you had to get."

"You could be out there for six months, depending on the weather. It means death if you aren't prepared."

"Mr. Smith, did you get everything on this list? It seems a lot of things. Where did this list come from?"

"Everything, ma'am, and the list came from the merchant."

Chapter Two

"*Miss Murphy,* I am going to the mercantile."

Rose smiled at Lachlan and said, "I'll go with you."

They passed hundreds of people loading goods into their wagons.

A man was heard shouting, "Hurry it up! We leave in the morning! It'll be dark by the time we finish loading the supplies if you don't get a move on it."

A gangly boy hollered back, "I'm hurrying as fast as I can, Pa."

A rooster crowed from a crate on a wagon. Chickens cackled. Mules brayed. Bells on harnesses jangled, hooves stamped as horses neighed hello to each other. The wind blew across the wagon tarps, sounding like shutters flapping on a window. Women roasted bread in heavy black cast iron pans around small campfires. The smell of beef stew and fresh bread wafted in the air. Rose couldn't help feeling hungry. She hoped she'd be able to create food with such tantalizing smells one day.

Lachlan stepped up onto the wide wooden porch of the mercantile and reached back to give Rose a hand up onto the high boardwalk.

The store was filled with people making purchases.

"May I help you?" The clerk peered at them from above his round spectacles.

"Yes, sir. I have a few items I need." He handed the clerk the crumpled paper.

"Let's see here. Just a small barrel of blackstrap molasses, a bolt of cloth, some needles and three spools of thread? Do you already have a shotgun and shells?"

"Yes, Sir."

"That's good. We ran out of shotguns and shells a week ago. You'll need them on the trail. I can help you with the rest of this list. Please choose your fabric from the bolts, ma'am."

Lachlan had already stocked the wagon with a bucket of axle grease, candles, waterproof matches, a butter churn, one hundred pounds of flour, one hundred pounds of rough bran, one hundred pounds of dried beans, a barrel filled with two hundred pounds of salt-cured bacon nestled in sawdust, fifty pounds of coffee, one hundred pounds of sugar, a sack of hard tack biscuits, a sack of cornmeal, a small bag of stick cinnamon, one hundred pounds of potatoes, a sack of dried raisins, one hundred pounds of dried meat, twenty pounds of rice, two hundred pounds of grain, and two huge barrels of water that could be replenished from streams.

"Will that be everything, sir?"

Rose was off examining the cloth she wanted, so she didn't hear Lachlan's addition to the list.

"Add a small bag of sweets, please."

Lachlan tucked the bag into his pocket and counted out the coins for the clerk.

"Thank you for your business, sir."

Carrying their packages, Lachlan took Rose on another shopping adventure. They arrived at an auction yard just in time to bid on the remaining milk cow, five chickens, and a scrawny goat.

"We're all set now, Miss Murphy," Lachlan said as he tied the goat and the cow to the back of their wagon.

He put tin pails in front of the animals for grain and water. The chickens would live in the crate they came in. He would like to have let them loose to find bugs, but he was afraid they would be gone by morning. Their freedom would have to wait.

That night, Owen and Willow came to visit. It was lovely to sit around the fire with company. Willow stared at the fire without speaking.

"I'm glad you decided to join us, Lachlan. It would have been mighty lonely without my little brother around." Owen smiled at Rose. "What a blessing God sent you a cook." Rose could see all eyes turn towards her. How would she respond?

"Actually, Owen, I'm a terrible cook. I'm looking forward to having lessons from Willow." This was the first time Willow looked fully at Rose and smiled.

This was their last night before they would be heading out on the trail, so they decided to retire early. Four in the morning would arrive far too soon. Lachlan extinguished the fire, then helped Rose into the wagon. "Good night, Miss Murphy. God bless you."

Rose awoke to the strangest sound. Someone was playing a bugle. Whoever it was didn't have the slightest idea how to blow it. The racket was horrible. Was it really four am already? Rose started to climb out of the back of the wagon and tumbled into Lachlan's arms.

"Sorry, ma'am. Didn't mean to startle you." Lachlan laughed. "It looked like you needed help. Didn't want you to fall."

Rose was embarrassed to be whisked away from the wagon steps but marveled Lachlan had such strong arms.

"Thank you, but I am perfectly capable of climbing down by myself."

Lachlan grinned at her as he said, "Why don't you meander over to Willow's wagon and watch how she prepares breakfast."

Willow's wagon was only five wagons behind theirs. It was the very last wagon on the train. Rose smiled as she greeted her new friend. She was surprised to see Willow smile back. She was even more surprised to hear Willow softly say, "Good morning, Rose."

Rose was so astonished she couldn't answer.

"I'll teach you to make cinnamon Johnnycakes, Rose."

Willow took a tin cup and filled it twice to the brim with cornmeal. She mixed in a bit of sugar and cinnamon, gradually adding water until it formed a thick paste. She dropped some bacon fat into a cast iron frypan that was already hot from the fire. She waited until the fat sizzled before dropping half cups of the cornmeal mix into the pan. The smell was heavenly. Rose wondered if she had ever tasted anything so good. Willow gave her about a dozen little cakes to take back for Lachlan.

The team of oxen had just been hitched to the wagon when Rose arrived with the Johnnycakes. "Guess what I know how to make now?"

As Lachlan appreciatively ate the gift, he asked if it was hard to make.

"No, it was so easy. I'm sure I can do it."

At 7:00 am, they heard another attempt at a bugle blast. This time it was accompanied by Captain Whittaker's shout of "Wagons Ho!" It was time to move out. The first wagons rumbled out. Being in one of the last of fifty wagons meant they had to wait. Lachlan rode his stallion up and down the train, making sure all was well. Ten soldiers rode beside the wagons. They had been hired to make sure folks were safe on the trail. Their muskets were loaded. This wasn't their first trail ride, and they knew more than they would ever say what perils awaited.

Rose wasn't sure if she should walk or ride in the wagon. She didn't want to overburden the animals, but Lachlan assured her that her one-hundred-pound contribution to the over two-thousand-pound weight of the wagon and supplies was not going to make a particle of difference. She decided for the start of the journey she was going to sit on the wagon seat and watch the land go by.

Every time Lachlan rode past on his powerful stallion, he tipped his hat, smiled, and said, "Howdy, ma'am."

My, he's a handsome man.

She quickly dismissed the thought. She didn't want to be distracted from her main goal of going to Oregon. It did seem like he rode past the wagon a lot, though.

Rose was daydreaming while waiting her turn to shoosh the oxen.

Rose couldn't help but wonder again, *Did I really hear from God to go West? The call of the West was strong. I had to answer it. I wonder what kinds of adventures I'll find on the trail?*

Just then Lachlan rode up. "It's our turn, Miss Murphy. Can you manage?"

Does he think I'm a child?

Rose took off the hand brake, just as he had shown her, and slapped the backside of the oxen with the ox goad. Even though Rose was trying to look confident in the seat, when the oxen lurched, she fell forward. Lachlan had the nerve to laugh.

"You'll get the hang of it soon."

He smiled as he rode off to check on the rest of the train. Watching the wagon in front of her, Rose noted several things.

I see why they call this thing a prairie schooner. It looks like a ship at sea. No wonder the cover had to be oiled to protect it from rain. I can see the wisdom in that. Dear God, please help me be a blessing to others on this wagon train. And please, help me learn how to cook. Thank You, Abba.

The first day on the trail was almost over. Camped by a quiet stream, they ate a quick supper of bread and cheese. After the tin dishes were washed and put away, Rose pulled her favorite book from her steamer trunk. She had lost track of how many times she had read it. Sitting on a stump by the fire, she opened it to her favorite passage, Ruth 1:16-17.

"But Ruth replied, "Don't urge me to leave you or to turn back from you. Where you go, I will go, and where you stay, I will stay. Your people will be my people, and your God my God. Where you die, I will die, and there I will be buried. May the Lord deal with me, be it ever so severely, if even death separates you and me."

She didn't mean to, but she sighed aloud. Hopefully Lachlan didn't hear her. She glanced up and across the fire, only to see he was looking at her. There was a strange look in his eyes she didn't recognize. Was it longing? Couldn't be. Rose blushed.

She quickly looked down at her Bible and tried to concentrate. Reading was impossible. She glanced up again. This time Lachlan was reading from his Bible that lay across his lap. The man looked so peaceful, too deeply engrossed in his reading to notice Rose studying his face. There was such a goodness in his features that drew her in. She wanted to know more about this kind, gentle giant of a man.

The fire crackled and snapped. A coyote howled in the distance. Rose swatted the ever-present mosquitos. She was mildly annoyed to see he was so deeply engrossed he was completely oblivious to the insects.

Her voice seemed to shatter the silence when she asked, "Mr. Smith, what are you reading?"

"Ma'am?"

"I'm sorry. I didn't mean to disturb you."

"That's quite all right, Miss Murphy," he smiled. "I sometimes get so caught up in the beauty of God's Word I forget where I am."

"You looked so taken in by what you were reading. What was it?"

Now Lachlan blushed.

"In Jewish culture, I heard a man is forbidden to read this book until he is thirty years old and about to marry."

"Why is that?"

"Well, I reckon it's cause it stirs up emotions in folks that can't be satisfied until marriage."

"Oh?"

"It's my favorite verse from Solomon's Song."

Pulling her shawl around her shoulders, Rose moved closer to the fire. She held her breath, waiting to hear Lachlan's voice. His deep, soothing voice read the passage with such emotion she was swept up in the beauty of it.

"It's from chapter eight verses six and seven of the Song of Solomon." He paused and looked at Rose, as if deciding if it was appropriate to continue.

"Set me as a seal upon your heart...as a seal upon your arm, for love is strong as death, jealousy is fierce as the grave. Its flashes are flashes of fire, the very flame of the Lord. Many waters cannot quench love, neither can floods drown it. If a man offered for love all the wealth his house, he would be utterly despised."

Lachlan looked up with misty eyes and said, "That's the kind of love I hope to find one day." His eyes held hers captive for a moment. She had to look away.

"Thank you for reading those verses to me. They're beautiful."

Lachlan poked the fire with a stick. Sparks flew in the air, mesmerizing Rose. They seemed to dance all the way to the stars.

"My Ma and Pa had a love like that," Lachlan said quietly.

"Where are they now?"

"They died thirteen years ago. Cholera."

"I'm sorry."

"I was ten years old. My brother Owen is ten years older than me. He took me in and raised me. I'm forever beholden to him for his kindness."

Silence enveloped them, except for the far-off songs of the coyotes.

"Miss Murphy, tell me about yourself."

Lachlan grabbed a small chunk of wood, pulled out a knife, and began to whittle. He figured he might as well make a spoon every night. They would come in handy if he ever had to barter for goods.

"I hardly know where to begin—it's such a crazy story. I was born in New York. My parents were wealthy, high society kind of people. Sadly, when I was four, scarlet fever struck. My parents and my infant brother died. It's a miracle I never got the disease. I was placed in an orphanage as I had no surviving relatives. My estate was held in trust until I reached the age of twenty-one. That was this past year."

"An orphanage? What was that like?"

Rose sat quietly, wondering what to say and how to say it. A verse went through her mind. *"May the words of my mouth, and the meditations of my heart, be acceptable in your sight, O Lord."*

She was quiet so long, Lachlan finally said, "It's okay. You don't have to tell me."

Rose smiled at the man sitting across the fire. Would her story sound unbelievable?

"I'm just trying to figure out how to say it. I've never said any of this out loud before."

From a nearby tree, an owl hooted. The crickets began their nightly serenade to the moon. Lachlan whittled, waiting for Rose to speak.

"I had a hard time not hating the woman who ran the orphanage. She beat the children for the slightest infractions. She fed us meagre amounts of food while she feasted daily. We watched her through the gilded glass French doors to her parlor. She would eat a whole chicken by herself. It was hard watching her. Sometimes we had so little to eat we would sneak out into the garden at night and eat the vegetables right out of the soil. We knew if we were caught, we would be beaten, but the hunger pangs drove us out there often."

"That's terrible."

"There's much worse. I pray God has mercy on her soul."

"Was she hard on you?"

"She knew I had an inheritance coming so that made me a bit of a favorite. I wasn't treated as severely as many others. Maybe she hoped I would make a donation one day."

"Did you?" Lachlan looked embarrassed. "Oh, my apologies. That's none of my business."

"It's okay. It's an honest question. I wanted to help those still trapped there, but I knew there was no point in making a donation. The money would have gone to Miss Shultz. It would have made her surroundings a bit more luxurious, and her waistline even more obese."

"That's terrible."

"I had to ask God to help me forgive her almost daily. It was horrible seeing innocent children beaten and starved because their chores weren't done acceptably. I got in trouble when I interfered."

"No wonder you were tempted to hate her."

"God, in His compassion, helped me forgive her. He let me see Miss Shultz through His eyes. He helped me love her."

"That's a miracle."

"I know."

They sat in silence for several moments.

"So, what did you do before you joined the wagon train and became my chief cook who will hopefully make the best Johnnycakes ever? I can't wait until you get the hang of how to make biscuits too."

Rose laughed. "I'll just have to remember when I make biscuits to use baking powder and not gun powder."

Lachlan laughed so hard it looked like he was about to cry.

"I was a teacher at an all-girls school."

"How did that come about? You were in an orphanage."

"Well, that's another miracle. When I was barely fourteen, a couple came to the orphanage. God put it on their hearts their daughter was there. When they met me, God confirmed to them I was to be theirs."

"That's amazing."

"I know. Only very young children were ever adopted. I had long given up hope of ever having a family."

"What happened then?"

"I moved into the most beautiful home I had ever seen and was treated like a princess. I literally went from rags to riches. I had a governess whose sole job was to educate me and make me a fine lady. My parents were grooming me to marry a doctor, lawyer, or a politician, anyone wealthy would do. They were excited when I was eighteen and expressed a desire to be a teacher."

"What happened then?"

"I will always be so grateful for my adoptive parents, the Murphys. They did everything they could to support me. My dreams became their dreams. We looked at schools, and they chose Marillac College in St. Louis, Missouri. They found a lovely women's boarding home where I continued to be pampered. That's my excuse for not knowing how to cook."

Lachlan laughed. "I'm sure you'll be a fast learner."

"After college, I had an apprenticeship at a girl's school in Independence. After the apprenticeship, I was offered a teaching position. I accepted. It was very prestigious and unheard of for a teacher just graduating to be offered a position there."

"So, why didn't you stay there?"

"I couldn't stay. I was there two years when I heard of the need for teachers out West, I felt God speaking to my heart to go. The Murphys were unhappy I wasn't following their script for my life."

"Did they eventually support your decision?"

"Sadly, no. My mother doesn't want to ever hear from me again. She is disappointed I am not choosing the life she wants for me."

"That must be hard."

Rose quickly changed the subject. "Thank you again for paying for my fare, Mr. Smith. I want you to know; however, you don't have to look after me. I am a grown woman. I can take care of myself."

The expression on his face seemed to say, I can clearly see you are a grown woman, but what he did say was, "That's amazing how God called you out West. I'm thankful I happened to be walking past at the exact moment you were being turned away."

"I'm thankful too, Mr. Smith. It was providential. If it wasn't for you, I'd be in St. Louis right now, with my parents trying to figure out which wealthy bachelor to introduce me to next."

Lachlan laughed again. His laughter somehow made her feel warm inside—and safe. It was the nicest laugh she had ever heard. *You must stop these crazy thoughts, Rose.*

Lachlan gave her a hand to climb up into the wagon. *What's wrong with this man? I can climb in a wagon by myself. Why does he seem to treat me like a child— or a porcelain doll? He seems to think I always need help. I am a grown woman— perfectly able to look after myself.*

Sunday, April 2, 1854

Dear Ma,
I plan to write you as often as I can. Hopefully, you will get this one day. So much has happened and we haven't even left Independence. We leave in the morning. I was denied passage on the wagon train because I was an unchaperoned female. Can you believe that? A kind young man heard my plight, offered to have me accompany him as his cook—I know, I can't cook—and he insisted on paying my fare. I confessed to him I can't cook, and he said his sister-in-law would be happy to teach me. Willow is a beautiful Sioux and looks like she may be having a baby any minute, so I need to get those cooking lessons soon.

I have learned so many things already. Mr. Smith seems to love teaching me. He said the most important thing on a wagon train is a sturdy wagon. I guess that makes sense, but I somehow never thought of that before. It has to be strong enough to withstand all kinds of weather. At the same time, it must not be too heavy or a team of oxen wouldn't be able to pull it all day, every day.

Mr. Smith said the wagons have to be about six feet wide and ten to twelve feet long. We picked up the supplies I requested today. He insisted on purchasing them because I am his cook. I imagine I'll be sleeping on top of the supplies, as the wagon is packed to the roof. Oh, I almost forgot. Don't worry. Mr. Smith will be sleeping under the wagon. He was very quick to explain that to me.

Water barrels, extra wheels, axles, and a crate of chickens will be attached to the outside of the wagon. Poor chickens. The wagon doesn't sound elegant, but I guess survival is more important than elegance. Obviously, there won't be any fancy chandeliers hanging in our wagon.

A prospector came by the wagon with a litter of puppies. He was asking one dollar each for the most adorable critters you ever saw. He planned to shoot the mother. He had no further need of her. I must have looked horrified, as he asked if I would like her. I looked at Mr. Smith, wondering what he would say. I now have the sweetest dog I have ever seen. Sadie adores me already. Maybe she knows I saved her life?

I love you, Ma.

Chapter Three

"Mr. Smith, how did Owen and Willow meet?

"Well, that's a funny story. It involves a mercantile and a man who needed to replenish his groceries daily."

"I think I've got the story line already," Rose laughed.

"Really? How does it go?"

"Let's see. Once upon a time, not that long ago, there was a beautiful baby girl born into the Sioux Nation. Her parents went on a hunting expedition, and after drinking contaminated water, died of cholera. The baby was alone—crying—abandoned on the side of a hunting trail. Thankfully, trappers came across the child, and wondered what to do with her. One of the trappers recalled a woman back at Fort Kearney just had a baby. Maybe she wouldn't mind nursing two babies? It was only an hour from where they found the child, so they decided they'd pay the new mother a visit. How am I doing with the story?"

"Great. Except it was Fort Boise."

"Really?"

Lachlan laughed. "Actually, I don't know which fort it was. But it's a great story. Keep going."

"When they arrived at the fort, there was a huge commotion. A woman was sobbing uncontrollably, seemingly unable to be comforted."

"What happened?"

"This was the mother the trappers intended to visit. Her baby son had just died of dysentery."

"That seems a bit too convenient."

"It's my story. So, the trappers told the distraught mother, let's call her Martha, about the baby they found. They opened their deer skin bundle and showed Martha the most beautiful baby girl she had ever seen. Her eyes were huge and brown, like a fawn's eyes. Her hair was silky, golden brown, the color of young willow branches, so Martha named her Willow. She fiercely loved that child."

"And then?"

"Willow grew up to be a beautiful young woman and got a job as a clerk at the mercantile."

"And then what happened?"

"A handsome, gentle giant of a man went into the store looking for flour one day, and to his surprise found a wife."

"Brilliant. I love it. It's so accurate."

"Yes, I know. Willow told me the story."

Lachlan laughed. "No wonder you had all the details. But if you already knew, why did you ask me how they met?"

"I wanted to hear a man-style version of what I consider a beautiful love story."

"Well, you missed some important details."

"Did I? Do tell me."

"You had to live with Owen to know what a profound effect Willow had on him. He was totally smitten. He even called me Willow a few times."

"That's hilarious."

"I know. It was funny watching how often Owen suddenly needed some item from the store. That went on for months. I'm sure Mr. Riley was thrilled. Owen was his best customer."

"What were your thoughts about your brother being so smitten?"

"I was genuinely happy for him. Willow was the kindest, gentlest woman I had ever met."

"What do you mean, was?"

"Well, now that I've met you, you've taken her place."

Rose blushed and suddenly found the fire fascinating.

"That's very kind of you, Mr. Smith."

They sat silently looking at the flames for quite a while.

Rose finally found her voice again.

"When did he ask if he could court her?"

"I couldn't believe how long he waited. Finally, after about five months of smiling at her every day and buying more groceries than he could possibly ever use, he invited her for a stroll. It lasted all afternoon; they went for dinner, and by dessert, they were engaged."

"I've honestly never seen a happier couple."

"Owen adores her. I think if anything happened to her, he would die of a broken heart."

"Let's pray God keeps them both safe."

"That's a good idea, Miss Murphy."

"What's a good idea?"

"To pray together. I don't know why I didn't think of it sooner."

"When is their child due?"

"I suspect it will be in about four months; around the time we reach the mountains."

"Is there a doula on the wagon train to assist her?"

"What's a doula?"

"A midwife. Someone who assists with a delivery."

"Owen asked if there was anyone with experience who could help deliver a child. Unfortunately, there was none."

"Would you speak to Owen and ask if I would be permitted to be with her?"

"Do you know how to help a birthing mother?"

"Well, one night a woman staying in the boarding house woke us all up with her screaming. We all ran towards the screams. We thought the woman was being killed."

"And…?"

"Well, Laurie's husband had passed away from scarlet fever just a few months before she came to stay with us. She rarely spoke, rarely ate. She was a wisp of a woman."

"Just a moment please, Miss Murphy."

Lachlan got up and put more logs on the fire.

"That should keep bears and cougars away. I don't want to be attacked in my sleep."

He stirred up the coals to get the new logs burning.

"Please carry on..."

"Laurie was so emaciated no one even knew she was with child. We did all we could to help mom and baby. Sadly, Laurie didn't have enough strength to deliver. She didn't have enough strength for life. We lost them both."

"That's a sad story. So, if they both died, how does that qualify you to be a doula?"

"I determined I would learn all I could about birthing so I would never find myself in that situation again."

"How did you learn?"

"I don't think I mentioned this before. When I was adopted, my parents already had an older adopted boy. Mark is a brilliant physician in Independence now. He let me assist him at the birth of several babies. I am pleased to tell you they all lived. I'm not a doula, but I do have some experience."

"Well, I thought God brought you here just to be my cook. It seems He brought you here to bless everyone around you."

"Will you tell them I can help?"

"Certainly. But why don't you speak to Willow yourself?"

"I'd feel better if you spoke with them."

"I'd be glad to, Rose."

Rose was startled.

This is the first time he's called me Rose. Does he even realize he said that? It seems the way he said my name—Rose—it was said lovingly. Odd.

Lachlan tried to coax a bit more warmth out of the fire. It was strange how days that were burning hot could end in such freezing cold nights. His face, lit up by the fire, was a picture of strength and gentleness. Somehow, just being in his presence made her feel safe.

"Are you cold? Would you like a blanket?"

Before she even had a chance to answer, Lachlan leaped to his feet as if a rattlesnake bit him. In a moment a blanket was being gently draped over her shoulders. Rose smiled up at the sweet man who obviously took his role of chaperone very seriously.

Sitting in the warmth of the fire until it was just embers, Rose was in awe at how expansive the sky was. The night was so dark the stars looked like brilliant diamonds that seemed to go on forever. It was too lovely a night to go to bed, but four am came very quickly. Reluctantly, she said, "I think I should get some rest now or getting up early will be impossible."

Lachlan held Rose by the hand as he helped her climb into the wagon.

"Night, Lachlan."

There was a pause before he spoke. He looked surprised she used his first name.

"Night, Rose."

Monday, April 3, 1854

Dear Ma,
We made excellent time yesterday, our first day on the trail. We followed the Little Blue River for about twenty miles. We only have just over two thousand more to go. So far, everything is going well. Mr. Smith takes such good care of everything—the animals, the wagon, the campsite—even me. I have the impression he thinks I'm very fragile. You know that's not true, right?

Last night was unbelievable. I have never seen such stunning and incessant lightning and thunder. The rain came down in torrents. The storm lasted the entire night. Hail stones, that sounded like they were the size of apples, hit the canvas cover on the wagon for hours and sounded like they were going to come through the canvas. It was nearly impossible to sleep. I felt sorry for Mr. Smith, sleeping under the wagon. I was tempted to invite him to sleep on the other bed, but I knew how improper that would appear, so I didn't.

We're crossing the Great Plains this week, and by traveling about fifteen or twenty miles a day, we hope to reach Fort Kearney in about a week. I heard we can get fresh vegetables there. I'm already getting tired of Johnnycakes and am longing for a carrot of all things.

I thought I knew how to make cinnamon Johnnycakes, but my first attempt was a disaster. Did you know even chickens don't like scorched Johnnycakes? My last batch was sort-of edible. Sadie loves anything I give her—scorched or not. She is so appreciative of scraps, pats and kind words. I think that was lacking in her other life.

Surprisingly, I'm getting good at making coffee. I've learned to make bread and molasses baked beans. I'm surprised how good my food is tasting—except when it's burnt. Mr. Smith has been trading his wooden spoons for different kinds of foods. We didn't bring onions, so it's nice that a spoon will buy five onions or a piece of dry codfish. Did you know codfish is delicious when boiled with rice?

The evenings are a lot of fun. Owen and Willow come by every night. Owen likes to tell stories around the campfire. A lot of them are about what a rascal his brother Lachlan was when he was little. It seems like every night we are collecting more people around our fire. I love it!

The train doesn't move on Sundays. We have a preacher along who tells us stories from the Bible. Because we stop in one spot on Sundays, that's also our washing day—if there's a river or lake nearby. Clothes and bodies are washed once a week—if that often.

There are quite a few children along on the trail. They are kept busy with chores: milking cows, making butter, and the endless chore of cleaning dust out of the wagons. Most have daily reading lessons. I'm tutoring a few of the children. It's fun having company as we are bumping down the trail. Sometimes I go to their wagons, and sometimes they come to mine. It keeps me from getting bored, otherwise the trail gets *mighty monotonous. Thankfully I have my set of McGuffey readers along. I thought I'd need them in my school. What I especially like about McGuffey is the readers start by teaching children the alphabet. By the time they are finished, they are reading literature I read in college. I like how this series covers all the bases for a complete language arts curriculum. It also teaches the basics of farming, history, and science. The stories teach good moral qualities, like kindness and compassion. Parents often come and sit around the campfire in the evenings to listen to the stories as well.*

Have you ever heard of black mouse pie? Probably not, because I invented the name. Cindy had so many mice attacking her oatmeal she somehow managed to trap them. Being the resourceful woman she is, and not wanting to waste all the mouse meat, Nellie made a black mouse pie. I don't think I could have eaten it if I was starving to death.

At night you can feel a chill in the air. It feels like winter is coming. Some of the trees have started to turn color in the highest parts of the trail. That gives me a feeling of dread. We left in April so we could be in Oregon before the snow. I don't think many are prepared for snow. I know I'm not.

Did I mention cholera comes from dirty water? It's actually a miracle we aren't all dead as most of the water we've seen has either a dead animal or human waste in it. I boil the water before we use it, but that doesn't always help. I'm trusting God to keep us safe.

Ma, if you get this letter one day, you know I was alive and able to send it to you. If we had known about the dangers that would face us, we would have wondered if coming on this journey in the first place was a sensible thing to do at all.
I love you, Ma.

That night, Rose found it impossible to sleep. Sadie usually slept quietly on the bottom of the bed, but tonight she was restless too. Instead of sleeping, she paced the narrow aisle—whining and growling. This wasn't like her at all.

In the middle of the night, Rose was surprised to hear voices coming from the front of the wagon.

"I told you the woman's rich."

"Shhh. Be quiet or you'll wake them."

"I's being quiet. Didn't ya' see the silk dress and the lace petticoat on that woman?"

Were they talking about her? As far as she could tell, she had the only silk dress on the wagon train.

"It's two in the mornin'. Do ya' think they's asleep?"

"Well, they better be, or we's in serious trouble. Didja' see the size of that man?"

"Yup, I wouldn't want to mess with him."

"What do ya' think she's got in that trunk?"

"I dunno, but I 'spect we's gonna be rich."

Rose didn't move. She barely breathed.

Lord, please wake Lachlan up.

The bonnet flap opened ever so slowly.

"Yup, she's sleepin'. I don't see the man."

"That's because he's behind you."

Lachlan grabbed both men by the scruff of their necks and yanked them off the wagon. He threw them on the ground and ordered them not to move.

"Rose, are you awake?"

"I am."

Rose sprang out of bed and looked out the back of the wagon.

"Fetch me some rope."

Rose quickly found some rope. Lachlan tied each man to a separate wagon wheel. Sadie jumped out of the wagon and growled at the intruders.

"Sadie, if they move, bite them. I'll deal with you both in the morning."

After that, Lachlan and Rose had the best two hours of sleep they ever had.

After the bugle sounded, Lachlan walked down the long line of wagons to talk to Captain Whittaker. By the time he got to the lead wagon, the sun had barely turned the edges of the sky pink. Captain Whittaker was about to take a blade to his face when Lachlan arrived.

"Morning, sir."

His face was covered in shaving cream when he poked it out the back of the wagon.

"Morning, Lachlan."

Lachlan watched, fascinated at how adept the trail boss was with a knife. He still hadn't quite got the hang of how to hold the knife, so every time he shaved there was blood.

"How can I help you?"

"I'm sorry to disturb you, sir, but there was an attempted robbery last night."

The razor paused momentarily.

"What happened?"

"A couple scoundrels attempted to climb into the back of my wagon. They said some nonsense about getting rich."

"Is that so? Then what?"

"I tied them both to a couple wagon wheels."

"Are they there now?"

"Yes, sir. Sadie's guarding them."

"Well, I guess we've lost today as a travel day."

"Why's that, sir?'

"We'll have to have a trial and decide what to do with these men. We can't have thieves among us."

"I agree, sir. It's not safe."

"Be so good as to tell the folks today is a rest day. They can wash, cook, sew, hunt, whatever needs doing. After lunch, the men will hold court and decide what happens to these ruffians."

Very good, sir."

'Spread the word the men will meet at your wagon after the noon meal."

"Yes, sir."

As they walked towards the prisoners, Rose asked, "What do we do with them until afternoon?"

"Well, the Christian thing to do would be to feed them. Didn't Jesus say love your enemies?"

Walking over to the prisoner, Rose checked to be sure his hands were still tied. The man's eyes looked wild as she tried to spoon oatmeal into his mouth. As soon as he had a mouthful, he spit it back into Rose's face. His words were venomous.

"You wretched woman. You've lived a pampered life. Had everything handed to you. You wouldn't know what it's like to be hungry and in want. I hope you rot in H---."

He didn't have a chance to finish. One blow from Lachlan knocked him out cold.

Rose went to the wash bucket to clean the oatmeal off her face.

Lachlan faced the other thief.

"I guess your friend wasn't hungry. Are you planning to spit your food out too?"

"No, sir. I'd be mighty grateful for some food."

"Your name is?"

"Jake, sir."

"And your friend?"

"His name's Jeb. He's my brother."

As Lachlan spoonfed the man, he questioned him about his intentions.

"So, why did you decide to visit my wagon?"

"It warn't my idea."

"Naturally. It's usually the other guy's fault."

"No, really. I didn't come on this here wagon train lookin' to rob folks."

"So, why did you go along with the plan?"

"Well, I kinda got pressured."

"How?"

"Well, Jeb paid my fare for this here wagon train. He said if I helped him, my debt'd be paid."

"Because of that, you thought it was a good idea to steal someone else's belongings?"

"Well, when you put it that way, I reckon it does sound pretty terrible."

"It doesn't matter how you put it. It sounds terrible."

That afternoon, Rose went to visit Willow because the women weren't welcome at the trial. The men folk came and stood around the two thieves. Wagon trains made their own laws and carried out their own justice.

"Men," Captain Whittaker said, "We need to draw up a constitution for this here wagon train—set some laws that we all must abide by— decide how to handle serious crimes like murder, rape, attempted rape, theft, and horse theft."

"Hang 'em or banish 'em all from the wagon train!" Clayton said.

"Should we have a judge and a jury to try the criminals, or do we all vote?" Jacob asked.

"We all vote. The choices are banishment or hanging." Captain Whittaker spoke with such authority there were no further questions.

"Okay, folks, now that we have decided on our constitution, we can vote on the matter at hand." The captain explained the situation. "These here varmints tried to rob Lachlan's wagon. What should we do?"

"Hang 'em!" one voice yelled out. Jake was visibly startled.

"Naw, they weren't stealin' horses. We should only hang horse thieves, rapists, and murderers."

"That's right. But they was climbin' into someone else's wagon to steal. We can't trust 'em."

The captain pulled on his suspenders and spit out a chunk of well-chewed tobacco before he spoke.

"Men, I suggest we let them take their wagon and get outta here."

That's when Jeb spoke up. His voice sounded pathetically whiny. "But you can't leave us alone out here. We don't have no maps. We don't know where we're goin'. We could die."

"Well, maybe you should have considered that before you decided to steal," someone said.

Captain Whittaker spoke up. "All in favor of cutting this riffraff loose say aye."

There was a chorus of ayes.

"Any opposers?"

"I oppose it. I think we should hang 'em," Clayton said.

"The ayes have it. You have half an hour to get your sorry backsides outta here."

Once they were untied, the men ran. Their wagon was out of sight within the hour.

Chapter Four

Rose awoke to a strange snorting sound. It was right outside the wagon. Lachlan's voice sounded far away, yet it still quietly commanded, "Rose, get on the floor. Keep Sadie with you."

Rose didn't argue or hesitate. She had learned to trust this man. He wouldn't be ordering her to do something unless he had a good reason.

As she lay on the wagon floor, the snorting snuffling sound got louder.

"Are you on the floor?"

"Yes."

"Stay down."

Rose held Sadie's head down.

"Shhhh. It's okay, girl."

Sadie whimpered, but didn't move. It seemed she knew Rose wanted to protect her. A shotgun blasted, then there was an eery silence. The snorting stopped.

Lachlan put his head in through the back flap and said, "It's okay, Rose. You can get up now. The bear's dead."

That night there was a roast bear feast in the camp. Harmonicas and guitars appeared out of nowhere. The whole camp danced and sang. That was the first time Lachlan danced with Rose. Watching Lachlan trying to square dance was probably one of the funniest things she had ever seen. It was obvious this was the first time he attempted square dancing. Somehow, he was a natural at waltzing. He held Rose as close as was proper for a gentleman, smiling into her eyes. It was a good thing Lachlan was holding her up, as those eyes made her swoon.

Rose hated to see people say goodnight and leave. It was the most fun she had in her life. When the last stragglers left, it was just her and Lachlan and a bear skin.

"I'll ask Willow to teach you how to cure the skin. When we go through the Rocky Mountains, you'll be mighty glad for the extra warmth."

"Lachlan…"

"Yes, Rose."

"I think the bear hide should be yours."

"Why?"

"You're the one sacrificing a warm bed so I can be on this wagon train. It doesn't seem right. You're always looking after me. You barely think of your own comfort."

"I'm fine, Rose."

"Wouldn't it be nice to have a furry blanket to keep you warm at night?"

He refused to keep it, saying as soon as he saw the bear, he thought what a fine, warm bed covering the hide would make for Rose.

Thursday, April 20, 1854

Dear Ma,

We arrived at Fort Kearney at dusk. There are five log houses perched on top of a hill. Even though we couldn't see a soul, I had the oddest feeling we were watched as our wagons rolled into town. We have traveled over three hundred miles from Independence. Captain Whittaker says we're making good time. He's trying to keep our morale up. It must be hard, because some are so tired of this journey. Today was very long and hot. People are exhausted—covered in dust. We still have to set up camp and cook a meal. You can tell when people are at the point of exhaustion. Emotions are on edge.

People bicker more— children cry easily. The wind is carrying the sounds of frayed nerves.

A saloon is sitting in the middle of nowhere. Strangest thing you ever saw. It looks like a strong puff of wind would knock it over. Maybe they hope a town will spring up around it. Lachlan said anyone who goes in there is doomed to lose everything they own. He said black jack and poker tables are never in the customer's favor. He also had no doubt disreputable men and women take up residence there. Sadly, in the dusk, I saw a few of our men making their way towards the saloon. I hope they still have a wagon in the morning.

Captain Whittaker had the wagons pull in closer when we got into a circle that night, as rumors of the Sioux Indians on the warpath unnerved him. It takes a lot to rattle that man, so this must be serious. The men were told to sleep with their loaded rifles beside their beds. It was unnerving to see a group of Sioux around the saloon. If they attacked, the folks knew the wagon train would have been nearly defenseless. Just so long as the Sioux didn't know that Independence had a shortage of gunpowder, we should be safe. We knew there were incidents where wagon trains were attacked. Many had been killed and scalped, wagons plundered, and set on fire. The captain knew a train of fifty or more wagons was reasonably safe, but one could never be sure. We are hovering at fifty.

The womenfolk weren't told about a possible attack. Most figured it out by the way their men behaved as they loaded their guns. I was surprised when Lachlan said he would cook dinner and bring it to me inside the wagon. I thought he was joking, but he was dead serious. While we sat in the wagon eating boiled potatoes and boiled beef jerky, Lachlan explained why he was concerned. He said as my chaperone he had the responsibility to bring me safely to my destination. He was worried if a Sioux warrior saw me, I would be snatched away. I laughed. He didn't.

Honestly. Does he really believe such nonsense? He looked at me so seriously I stopped laughing.

There has been a tragedy. Usually, the animals are kept at the center of the wagons. Last night, the wagons were so tight together, a few of the animals were tethered outside the circle. The animals must have sensed something was up as they bawled half the night. As Michael collected his animals, something—perhaps a snake—caused them to stampede. He was knocked over. Because the reins were wrapped around his arm, he was dragged.

Owen found the team by the river, quietly drinking and eating as if nothing had happened. Michael was still tethered to the reins, dead. Michael's wife and children were beside themselves with grief. Amanda was afraid to continue the journey West without her man. How could she look after everything? Some of the men promised to help. It was a kind offer, but they had their own animals and families to care for. It really was impossible for them to do anything more. I was just getting to know Amanda. She and her children came to listen to my fireside stories often. I felt so sad for her.

Before I tell you the rest of the story about Amanda, I must take a small rabbit trail so you will understand her predicament.

I often walk beside the wagon for exercise and to see the countryside. I somehow feel I'm helping the animals not have to carry so much weight. Sadie loves to run in circles around me, chasing after anything that looks interesting. Have I mentioned what a good hunter Sadie is? She loves catching prairie rabbits and chickens and presenting them to us. I think she wants to be a contributing member of her family.

Before we started on this journey, I thought the wagon wheels looked so sturdy nothing could ever happen to them.

They were carved from wood and had strong metal bands around them. I didn't understand why we had to carry extra wheels. It seemed so unnecessary. While we were still in Nebraska, not too far along on the trail, the metal rims started to separate from the wooden tires. The heat of the sun made the wood shrink. When it shrinks, the metal rims are too big and roll off. The men now have to take the wagon wheels off every night to be soaked in water in a nearby river or a lake to keep the iron rims from rolling off during the day.

Removing the wheels at night, carrying them to and from water, then putting them back on in the morning, has added to the men's list of chores. I don't know how they do it. I couldn't do it. Every day I understand more why an unaccompanied female could never survive on this trip. I was so naïve. I can't imagine having to do all the work Lachlan does. I have such a high level of respect for him.

I'm not walking much these days. The sun is too scorching hot. Several pioneers from our group insisted on walking and have died from exposure. It's a sobering lesson not to take life for granted. Life hangs in the balance easily out here. Graves are dug often. The hardest ones are the children's graves. There are so many freak accidents it's hard to believe. Someone said they heard one out of every five children don't survive this trip. Such horrible statistics.

One of the loaded rifles discharged in the night—maybe a rat ran over it—and a little boy was killed instantly. Another was riding on the front of the wagon, fell off, and was crushed by the wheel. There are so many gruesome stories. I feel so unprepared for all of this. I miss you and the girls terribly. I miss my soft bed, fine china, delicious meals, and elegant clean dresses. My clothes look like I was in a mud fight. If I could, I would go back to Independence in a heartbeat.

Several folks, who didn't have an extra wheel, were left behind to fend for themselves. The wagon train couldn't wait. If we waited, it could mean death for all of us. We have to get through the Rocky Mountains before it snows. My friend Amanda, and her precious children, were among those left behind. I wonder if they will live. It's brutal to think about. I pray God protects them.

So many crazy things have happened here. There was a black bear in the camp two days ago. It was actually hilarious. Someone left an empty bean pot by their wagon. There was a large wooden spoon in it that must have still smelled like baked beans. It was the funniest thing I ever saw. The bear lumbered off with the wooden spoon sticking sideways out of its mouth.

My lips have blistered and split in the hot dry air. Lachlan said I must put axle grease on my lips. Axle grease? How ridiculous. I am painfully aware I'm a long way from the city. As I am writing this, I am sitting on the seat of the wagon as it lurches down the trail, with axle grease on my lips.

Indians seem to like using the canvas top of the wagons for target practice. Other than that, things are kind of boring.

I love you, Ma.

Rose awoke the next morning with a horrible toothache.

It's crazy how quack doctors at the forts prescribe all kinds of silly things — rum, opium (Laudanum), castor oil, and whiskey. One woman had an upset stomach so a "doctor" told her she must drink an expensive elixir he prescribed. I think it was half camphor and half whiskey. It must have tasted disgusting. The woman drank the bottle of "medicine" and eventually got better, but I'm sure it had nothing to do with the medicine.

Before Lachlan went to collect the oxen from the field and the wheels from the river, he pulled out a flask of whiskey, prescribed by a quack doctor presumably, and told her if she had some it would help take away the pain. Lachlan forgot to specify how much "some" was.

Rose was supposed to get the fire going and have breakfast ready by the time he arrived with the wagon wheels and had yoked the oxen. Rose decided she had lots of time to prepare breakfast. She sat on her bed and had a swig of the medicine. It didn't help. She was still in pain. Perhaps she didn't have enough. She took another swig. The pain was still there.

How much medicine does it take to kill the pain?

When Lachlan got back, there was no roaring fire or breakfast bread waiting. Rose was nowhere to be seen.

"Rose?"

He looked in the back of the wagon and was shocked to see Rose lying on the wagon floor with her legs up on the bed. The empty flask of whiskey lay beside her. Sadie was curled protectively beside her.

"Rose?"

Rose slowly turned and looked towards the voice. She grinned at Lachlan.

"You were right," she giggled. "The medicine did take away the pain."

That was the last thing Rose remembered until evening. As soon as Rose looked out the back of the wagon, Lachlan sprang to his feet and rushed to help her climb down.

"Steady as she goes," Lachlan laughed.

"This isn't funny, Lachlan James Smith. The medicine you gave me was deadly."

"You weren't supposed to drink the whole flask, Rose Caroline Murphy."

Rose sat on a stump, feeling the warmth of the fire. It was lulling her to sleep again. She felt like she was going to fall over at any moment. Lachlan noticed and sat beside her to steady her.

"How are you feeling?"

"I have a fierce headache."

"Here, drink some water."

Lachlan held a flask of water to her lips.

"The fresh air will help. Are you hungry? I've got some beans and rice."

The thought of food made Rose feel nauseated.

"No, thank you."

"Is the toothache gone?"

Rose realized with surprise her tooth didn't hurt any more.

"Yes, it's gone."

"There, you see, the medicine worked."

The fire crackled happily. The evening was so peaceful.

That's when the arrow struck the side of the wagon.

"Rose, quick. Get in the wagon."

She wasn't traveling fast enough for Lachlan so he grabbed her around the waist and pretty much threw her into the wagon. Sadie jumped in behind her.

"Stay down."

An arrow flew past him and landed in the tarp exactly where Rose had stood moments before. Lachlan rolled under the wagon and grabbed his rifle. He kept one there just in case. Other men could be seen under their wagons.

Thankfully, there was enough gunpowder to make the Indians think they had no chance against this wagon train. A long howl was heard, a sign of retreat from the chief.

Almost an eternity later, when the dust from the horses' hooves settled, Lachlan crawled towards the man moaning under the next wagon. Jude's face was contorted in agony. An arrow shattered his shoulder. Two other men also crawled under the wagons towards the man. As soon as he thought Jude was in good hands and there was nothing else he could do, Lachlan hurried to check on Rose.

"Rose, are you okay?"

Silence.

"Rose?"

Looking frantically in the wagon, he muttered, "Did an Indian warrior steal Rose?"

Sadie sat on the floor whining. This didn't look good.

"Dear God, please keep Rose safe."

He didn't want to panic, but where was she? He climbed into the wagon. Maybe she fainted?

"Dear God, please don't let any harm come to Rose."

Just then, Rose climbed into the front of the wagon. She was shocked to see Lachlan standing in the back of her wagon. They stared at each other in surprise.

"Lachlan, what are you doing in the wagon?"

"What were you doing *out* of the wagon?"

"I heard a child crying."

"Was the child okay?"

"No. Not at all."

"What happened?"

"His mother had an arrow stuck in her shoulder. The child was screaming. The mother was crying. She was in agony. Her husband was trapped under the wagon.

"So, what did you do?"

"I did the only sensible thing there was to do."

"…and that was?"

"I prayed. I asked God for wisdom and strength."

"Why did you need wisdom and strength?"

"To get the arrow out."

"Did you get it out?"

"Yes."

Then Rose did an unexpected thing. She burst out crying. Lachlan had little experience with crying women so was at a loss as to what to do.

Rose flung herself on the bed. Her sobs became louder, from somewhere deep within her soul. The sound was painful.

"Rose, what's wrong?"

"I want to go home."

"Rose, I'm so sorry."

"I hate it here," she said between sobs. "This is not at all what I expected."

"I don't see how you can go home now."

"If we see a wagon train heading east, I want to join them."

"I'll speak to Captain Whittaker in the morning. I'm sorry, Rose."

Lachlan tried to sleep, but it evaded him. He prayed out loud.

"Dear God, please have Rose reconsider this idea of going back to Independence."

Chapter Five

"*Lachlan, I saw twelve* wagons heading back East. Why did the man in the lead wagon stop and talk to you? What did he say?"

"The folks only made it as far as Fort Bridger, Wyoming, and decided it was just too hard. Their wagon train had over fifty wagons. Twelve are all that remained."

"What happened?"

"Cholera wiped out most of their train. They burned the cholera infested wagons and turned around."

"That's horrible. They must feel defeated. I'm sure they had so many dreams."

"They'll be fine. Most folks are pretty resilient."

"Do you think many of our folk will turn around?"

"I reckon so. Do you still want to go back to Independence?"

Rose saw the questions in Lachlan's eyes. Was she strong enough for this trip? Could she trust God to take her safely to Oregon? Was the lure of the sophisticated life she had known too strong a pull? Would she choose to go back to all that was familiar?

He didn't wait for an answer. "Rose, I know you are strong and determined. But is this more than you bargained for?"

"In all honesty, I wonder at times. Did I really hear God directing me to go West? Sometimes I miss my fine clothes, the elegant homes, the delicious dinners. It's funny the things you miss when you can't have them. I would love to have soup in a china bowl. I would love pure, fresh water served in a clean crystal glass. I didn't expect it to be so rough and dirty out here. I want to go back to all that's familiar. I understand why people turn back. This isn't what the advertising led me to believe it would be like."

"The advertising from the wagon train companies?"

"Yes. It's not what they said—"

"What did you expect?"

"I have a brochure in my trunk. I'll get it."

Lachlan whispered, "Dear God, you know I want to go on to Oregon, to start a new life there. I want it so bad I can taste it, but if she chooses to go back, I could never abandon her. She couldn't travel alone."

"It says, "Those who crossed the plains. never forgot the ungratified thirst, the intense heat and bitter cold, the craving hunger and utter physical exhaustion of the trail... But there was another side. True, they had suffered, but the satisfaction of deeds accomplished, difficulties that were overcome more than compensated, and made the overland passage a thing never to be forgotten."

"That doesn't sound like they painted a lovely picture, Rose."

"That was written by a pioneer. I know the brochure said it would be hard, but I didn't expect it to be *THIS* hard. I thought it would just be a great adventure. There's more in the brochure. It says,

"You can't leave too early in the year or there won't be grass for the animals and they'll starve. You can't leave too late or there's danger of freezing to death in a brutally cold winter."

"I guess I should have suspected from that it would be hard."

"Rose, I will respect whatever you choose. If you choose to go back, I'll go with you."

Rose was surprised to hear that. Was Lachlan really willing to give up his dream to protect her? What kind of man was this? She could never jeopardize his dreams—his very life.

A wagon traveling alone, or even in a small group, would be an easy prey for wild animals and hostile Indians.

Rose looked at this man who was willing to do anything to protect her. She longed to go back, but she realized with surprise she longed even more to be with this gentle, giant of a man. She had never felt so cared for—so safe and protected—in all her life.

"Lachlan, I would never ask you to give up your dreams for me. I'm going on to Oregon."

Lachlan looked deeply moved. "Rose, I hope you realize your strength, hope, and courage for this trip need to come from God. If you depend on your own feelings, your own grit and strength, it will be too hard. You will fail. One day at a time…"

"I know."

"Rose, this is one of my favorite Bible verses. I think it will encourage you. John 15:5 says,

"I am the vine, you are the branches. If a man (anyone) abides in Me, they will bear much fruit. For without Me you can do nothing."

God loves you, Rose. He doesn't expect you to do life without Him."

Thursday, May 25 1854

Dear Ma,

We left Fort Kearney, and followed the Platte River for over six hundred miles to Fort Laramie. That took us over a month. The thunderstorms have made traveling treacherous. There's mud everywhere. The wagons are sliding all over the trail. I was walking every day, but I'm not walking in this mud. It's too slippery and dangerous. You should see my clothes!

Well, I'm not sure if this will come as a surprise to you or not, but today I was ready to pack my steamer trunk and head back to Independence. The monotony and the hardships were getting to me. I honestly didn't see how I could go on. Lachlan said if I was going back, he was going with me. I couldn't let him give up his dreams to protect me so I told him I'm going on to Oregon.

It's funny, when I told Lachlan I was going on to Oregon. I swear he wanted to hug me. He looked like he was holding

himself back. The crazy thing about that is, I didn't want him to hold back. It's a good thing one of us has a sensible mind.

My survival cooking lessons with Willow went well until recently. She's been so sick she hasn't been up to giving me lessons for over a week. She's having terrible nausea. From what I can tell, this has been a hard pregnancy.

Ma, I have discovered the key to a man's heart. It's food. I can't believe how appreciative Lachlan is of my cooking. He loves my potato cakes. The recipe is so easy. You just mix the following ingredients and drop them by tablespoons onto a hot frypan. You need six potatoes, grated and peeled (I like to use the peels), one teaspoon salt, half a cup of milk, two eggs, and a cup of flour. If you come out West, I'll make them for you. Bring the girls. They would love them. Oh wait, you would all have to make this treacherous journey. Never mind. I'll just send you my favorite recipes.

We have Johnnycake often. It's delicious with beans. It's so easy to make. You need two eggs, two cups of sour milk, one half cup flour, two tablespoons molasses, one teaspoon salt, two cups cornmeal, one teaspoon baking powder, and two tablespoons butter. You mix all the ingredients then bake it in a Dutch oven over the fire until it's cooked. I think Johnnycakes is Lachlan's favorite.

Beef or buffalo jerky is surprisingly easy to make. You just have to slice the meat into very thin strips, going with the grain of the meat. I'm not sure why that's important, but Willow stressed it. I'll take her word for it. The strips have to be baked over a fire until dry. That's it. I make jerky on days we are in camp for the day. Willow taught me how to pound wild berries into the meat before it's dried to make it more delicious.

One of my favorite recipes is fry bread. On days we stay in camp, I make enough for the week. It gets a bit hard towards *the end of the week, but softens when it's dipped in stew. Here's the recipe: Four cups flour, one quarter cup shortening—I use bacon fat—four teaspoons baking powder, three-quarters cup of milk, one teaspoon salt, and oil or fat for frying. If the dough is too thick or thin, Willow said to play with it until it feels just right. It can also be made into a dessert if you put milk, cinnamon, and berries on top.*

There's so much to learn before you even start cooking. One of my lessons was how to milk a cow. I miss getting my milk delivered in a bottle. Did you know you must make sure your hands are warm before you touch any part of the cow, otherwise you are in danger of being kicked? I found that out the hard way.

The butter making lesson was surprisingly easy. The only difficult part is trying to keep Sadie's nose out of it. You just put the milk in the butter churn—it was wise Lachlan bought one when he purchased the supplies—and you keep turning the paddle until it refuses to turn any further. I was getting tired of Johnnycakes. They have taken on a whole delicious new life smeared with fresh butter and wild berries.

Cheese is easy to make. It's a good way to use the two gallons of milk we get from our cow and the goat each day. We are getting so much we have been sharing. Willow showed me how to gently heat the milk in a pail on the fire until it's blood warm. Rennet is needed to make cheese, so I use a flask made from a cow's stomach because it has rennet in it. I had no idea. I pour the hot milk into the stomach flask and wait. After it's been left a few hours, I pour it out, break up the curds, and mix them with salt. I wrap the curds in a cloth and put them in a round wooden frame called "the follower." (Thankfully, Lachlan had the good sense to buy one of those also). The curds are pressed in the follower.

The cheese is usually aged for at least two months before it can be eaten. Willow said this is to be sure the good bacteria has overpowered the bad bacteria. We don't have the room or the time to wait. It's stored on a salty plate, covered in a cloth to keep flies off, and turned every day—or when I remember. The longer we wait to eat the cheese, the sharper and dryer it becomes. Lachlan says my cheese is the best he has ever tasted. Such a kind man. Enough about cooking. It just makes me miss your fabulous meals.

The landscape is honestly getting boring. It's taking over a month so far to cross Nebraska and every day looks the same. It's a bit unnerving, as I keep thinking I've seen the same rock or tree already. It makes me feel like we're traveling in circles. This is a joke, so don't be alarmed. Lachlan said he would almost welcome an Indian attack just to relieve the monotony.

Captain Whittaker said we will be seeing some landmarks soon. He said there are rocks called Courthouse Rock, Chimney Rock, and Scott's Bluff that will be interesting to see. I think he intended to keep our spirits up with that news. That was over a week ago and still no landmarks in sight. His news is getting old.

This is sad news. Because folks have been told there is a danger of Indian attacks, people bought up almost all the ammunition at the last fort. Our fifty wagons now carry about two hundred pistols and rifles, I'm sure nearly a ton of lead, and about a thousand pounds of gunpowder. This is the sad part. A fire somehow got out of control from a campfire and three wagons blew up from all the gunpowder. There were no survivors. It was horrible.

This is another sad story. A man saw a bear nosing around his wagon, so he quickly reached for his rifle. Unfortunately, he grabbed it muzzle first and the firearm went off. He leaves behind a frantic wife and several small children.

There is talk of a number of wagons turning around and heading back to civilization. It would be very hard for the women to continue without their menfolk so they plan to return to Independence. I don't blame them. None of this is what they signed up for. I couldn't do this trip without Lachlan. I can certainly see why unaccompanied women are denied passage on the wagon train. It's hard enough even with a man.

We've had another issue. Snakes. They are everywhere. Most of them are not venomous, but the ones that are will kill you in about twenty minutes. I guess the good news about that is people have time to make their peace with God before they stand before Him. The dangerous snakes are cottonmouths, copperheads, and rattlers. Honestly, Ma, like I said, they are everywhere. They are in the bushes, in the rocks, on the flats, on hillsides, in the marshy wetlands, in the desert areas, in the canyons and on the hills. Several folks have died from bites.

I must tell you something amazing I discovered about Sadie. She warns me when anything dangerous is around. She walks in front of me so I can't go any further and growls. She has kept me from stepping on so many snakes. What a blessing God brought her to us!

I thought we were hearing coyotes every night, but Lachlan said there are wolf packs too. Both critters howl, but when we hear yipping and barking Lachlan said that's coyotes. That man knows so much. I'm learning much more than I ever wanted to know. The howling gets worse when any dogs in the camp decide to howl back. The singing is deafening. Sadie has to be tied up at night, because if she chose to chase any wild critters, she would most likely be killed. She is learning we don't appreciate her howling in the night.

Getting up at 4:00 am every day makes a body bone weary. I feel tired all the time. I think what Lachlan said to me today makes a lot of sense. He said I can't do this alone. I realize I desperately need God to strengthen and hold me—to walk with me—to lead and guide. I guess that's obvious, but I was trying to keep up in my own strength. Do you ever do that? I was kind of asking God to wait close by me in case I got desperate, but meanwhile, I would try to handle things on my own. How stupid.

We camped outside Fort Laramie, and the next day experienced a hilarious monotony breaker. Who would have suspected Fort Laramie had paint? It seemed like a gift from Heaven. The monotony was stopped for a few hours as people painted messages and mottos on the canvas on their wagons. Some got a bit crazy and spattered paint on each other. We must have looked like a pretty wild, colorful bunch of savages. Sadie and the other dogs managed to get into the paint. They looked hilarious.

Lachlan boldly painted "ABIDE IN CHRIST" on one side of the canvas, and "JESUS LOVES YOU" on the other. I painted hearts and flowers around his messages. I wish you could see it. It's quite lovely, if I do say so myself.

Several had messages like, "OREGON OR BUST!" Some got so inspired they painted the wood on their wagons. A few folks looked like there was more paint on them than their wagon. We must have looked like the rainbow wagon train. I must say the paint made a very mundane day quite fun and has boosted the morale.

This was an unusual thing that happened a few days ago. While walking beside the wagon, I saw a dead raccoon. Sadie went over to investigate, and we were both startled to see a round little baby raccoon toddle towards us. Her little legs looked too short to carry her chubby body. She wobbled towards Sadie, who surprisingly, started to treat the baby as if she were her puppy. She picked up Ruby—that's what I named her—by the scruff or her neck, and carried her back to *our wagon. Once she was on the wagon floor, Ruby looked imploringly at me, with an expression that said, "Please, ma'am, do you have any milk to spare?" The look on her face was priceless.*

Sadie and Ruby are now inseparable. You should see how they sleep. It's adorable. Sadie curls up and Ruby plunks down and snuggles into the middle of the curl. I would not want to see anyone try to keep those two apart. During the day they romp and play together.

I am honestly so tired I can hardly think. The oil in the lamp is getting low, and I don't want to go outside in the dark looking for more. Who knows what's prowling around out there. I'm praying God holds you and the girls close to His heart. Thank you for your prayers. I can feel them. We are going to have a heap of catching up to do when we meet in Heaven one day.

I love you, Ma

Chapter Six

Lachlan gripped his coffee cup to keep his hands warm. It was funny how after a scorching hot day, the night brought a chill to the open prairies. Rose chuckled at the paint splotches still on his face and clothes.

"Why are you laughing, Miss Rose?"

"You look so funny in pink and purple."

"You look funny with red spots on your face."

"Red spots?"

"Paint."

"Oh. Phew. You had me worried."

"Why?"

"My parents' scarlet fever started with red spots on their faces."

An owl could be heard in the distance, not hooting the way most owls do, but screeching. Its' screams got the wolves howling.

"Sadie, don't even think of howling—"

"Rose, are you warm enough? Would you like me to get you the bear skin?"

Rose sat on her stump across the fire from Lachlan.

"I'm fine. Thank you."

I'm so grateful for this man. He takes such good care of me. He works tirelessly. How blessed I am God brought me and this man together for this journey.

"Lachlan, thank you for all you do to keep us safe."

"Mmm hmm."

Rose was surprised at his reply. Lachlan just stared into the fire. He seemed preoccupied. His thoughts were obviously elsewhere. He didn't seem to have heard Rose. There was something on his face she didn't recognize. Worry. That man never worried. Rose decided to distract him with small talk.

"Lachlan, did you know the Oregon trail is the longest trail on this continent?"

"Mmm hmm."

"That's crazy how it meanders over two thousand miles."

"Mmm hmm."

"I read in a brochure it starts in the East by the Missouri River, goes through the wildest terrain a body ever saw, then ends up by the Columbia River in Oregon in the West."

"Mmm hmm."

"Over two thousand miles of rugged terrain; everything from deserts, to deep valleys and high mountains. I didn't realize it would be so wild."

Rose could see her "small talk" hadn't helped one iota. The deep worry lines between his eyes were something she had never seen before. He just kept staring into the fire. What could be the matter?

Finally, he spoke.

"Tomorrow, we have to cross a wide river."

"We've crossed wide rivers before, Lachlan."

"Not like this one. I pray we make it."

Lachlan didn't mean to cause alarm, the words just slipped out before he could stop them.

"What do you mean?"

"Oh, nothing," Lachlan said calmly, nonchalantly—but Rose could see the concern in his eyes.

"Rose, I've been out with an Indian scouting party all afternoon. We rode for miles—"

His voice trailed off.

"What happened?"

"We tried to find a safe place to cross—"

"And?"

"There was none."

"I'm sure we'll be fine."

Lachlan didn't mention the water was too deep and the currents flowed way too fast for a wagon to cross safely. God would have to provide a miracle.

The next morning, Rose was shocked to see the river they had to cross. No wonder Lachlan had looked worried. The river was swollen with the spring run-off. Three feet was the maximum depth a wagon should be plunged into. This appeared much deeper. There were no other options but this spot. The rest of the places looked even deadlier.

It was disheartening to see the river bank littered with piles of supplies others had left behind. There was an iron safe, furniture, anvils, a plow, bookcases, and crates of books. Rose didn't understand why there was such a huge pile of goods, until the wagon that went into the water just ahead of theirs immediately sank to the bottom of the river. The weight of the wagon pulled it down.

Men stood up to their chests in the raging waters to guide the wagon. Supplies had to be thrown into the river until the wagon was light enough to float. It was horrible to watch. The oxen were still yoked to the wagon, frantically
swimming for their lives against the current. Horses snorted and churned the water with their hooves. It was nearly impossible to keep the chickens, goats, and pigs from drowning. The wagon lurched sideways, looking like a ship about to capsize. When all looked lost, the schooner righted itself and began to float.

As Rose surveyed the piles of provisions lying on the river banks and floating down the river, she wondered how people decided what to leave behind. Everything on the trail meant survival. It must have been hard to choose what to abandon.

Folks had to determine if oil or flour was more valuable. Could they keep the oil lamps to have light at night, or should they keep the bag of oatmeal? Squabbles broke out, as men wanted to keep wagon wheels and women insisted on keeping food. Children cried. The scene was a chaotic mess.

Rose hugged her friend Emily as she stood crying by the bank of the river. Her precious wedding gifts brought all the way from

New York were in that pile. Some had already floated down the river. All the beautiful things she had saved for years and brought for her own home were gone. That's when Rose realized the contents of her own trunk were going to present a huge problem.

Friday, May 26, 1854

Dear Ma,

I can't believe I'm alive. Yesterday was the worst day on the trail. It was brutal in so many ways. We arrived at Fort Laramie last night. I had heard it was nicknamed Fort Sacrifice. I thought that was such a strange name. Today I understand why it's called that.

There was a mercantile with so much goods, people went wild purchasing things. Honestly, I have never seen such a vast array of things to buy. The merchants kindly kept the store open for us, even though it was way past their closing hour. The folks thanked them profusely for their kindness. The merchants insisted it was no trouble at all.

When we arrived at the North Platte, I was horrified. Ma, you would not have believed that river. It looked incredibly deep and swift. That's because it was. My thoughts varied from, "You've got to be joking," to "I think we're going to die."

It was sad, Ma. Many had to discard valuable goods. There were piles of supplies discarded by the banks of the river. My friend Emily stood crying as her wedding gifts were given to the pile and to the river. People had to part with cherished heirlooms, wagon parts, and more. The women insisted food be kept, and the men wanted wagon parts. The women said you can't eat a wagon wheel and without food we'd starve. The men reasoned if the wagon needs a wheel, and you can't travel, you're also dead. The immediate need for food won.

So—Fort Laramie is known as Fort Sacrifice because so many precious items had to be abandoned. It's a shame unscrupulous merchants take advantage of folks and sell them way more than they need. Travelers are at their mercy. Merchants have inflated supply lists and inflated prices to match. They persuade people to buy way more than they need, fully knowing it will cause them grief as their animals wear out sooner, or their wagons are too heavy to cross swollen rivers. These store owners obviously don't care that people's lives are at stake. The gold rush prospectors and the Oregon Trail pioneers must seem like a gullible gift to these horrible people. This explains why while we were still in Independence, the list of supplies needed was so huge. I'm thankful for it now, as we have helped feed many people, but it was still unscrupulous of the merchants.

This is a truly terrible thing. I heard after the wagon trains cross the Platte River, many of these despicable merchants from Fort Laramie come and collect what people discarded. They haul them back to the fort, then sell them again at great profit to unsuspecting travelers. Here we thought they were so kind to keep the store open for us. I hate to say this, I know it sounds terrible, God forgive me, but I'm wondering if there's a special place in Hell for people like that.

The bottoms of all the wagons had to be caulked with tar so they would be water tight. We spent hours tarring all the wagons. I'm not sure what the point of caulking the bottoms was, as most of the wagons immediately sank to the bottom of the river. Almost everything in the wagons was soaked anyway.

That raging river nearly capsized our wagon. The oxen were so panicked they nearly drowned. Their eyes rolled back in their heads so they looked like they were possessed. The water was so deep and swift it was scary, and you know I don't scare easily. I heard later that if a river is deeper than three feet, don't even attempt it. Someone should have told us that before.

I sat in the wagon with Sadie and Ruby as we plunged into the river. As water rushed into the wagon, that was the scariest experience of my life. Ruby screamed, which startled me. I had no idea raccoons could scream. Most of my attention during the river crossing was focused on trying to calm a hysterical baby raccoon. Poor Sadie was beside herself. Her pleading eyes said, "Please, will you help my Ruby?" I decided to wrap Ruby in a cloth, maybe she would find that comforting, and hold her close to my heart so she could hear it beating. I heard puppies are comforted by that. That seemed to calm her somewhat.

As the water poured in, my clothes were drenched. The wagon was soaked. Thankfully, Ruby fell asleep beside Sadie, piled on a sack of oats high up in the wagon. The only noise breaking the silence was Ruby's deep purring sound. How she slept through all the commotion was a mystery. Being soaked really was the least of my troubles. My inheritance was the issue. I didn't want to tell anyone, but I had to. My trunk was too heavy for the river crossing. It couldn't stay in the wagon.

I had all my inheritance money put into gold bars, and hid the bars under my dresses and blankets in the trunk. When I told Lachlan what was in the trunk, he promised he'd get it across for me if he had to carry it above his head. That's exactly what he did. That wasn't the first time he carried my heavy trunk as if it was full of feathers. My hero.

The worst part of the day was when the wagon ahead of us capsized. Ned was trapped under it. By the time the men could right it, he had drowned. I watched it all. I heard Ned's wife screaming hysterically and saying she's heading back to Independence in the morning. I can't say I blame her. A couple other folk are turning around with her. They said this whole trip is just too hard. They can't stand it any longer. There's that gnawing feeling in my belly again, Ma. I want to turn around too, but I've given Lachlan my word that I'm going to Oregon, and I'm a woman of my word.

As we traveled today, we saw burned out wagons from Indian attacks. I wonder if that's why Willow is so shy? I wonder if she thinks people blame her for the atrocities. She had no choice being born a Sioux Indian. It's no different than being born Scottish or African or anything. Who cares? People are just people. I know that the destruction we saw has nothing to do with her. She's so sweet, gentle, and kind. I've never met a finer woman—well, besides you, that is.

I think I forgot to tell you what happened at the last lake we stopped at. No one is confessing to this crime. We all suspect it was a young man who has mental issues. It was the men's bath time. The men's clothes were left lying on the lake shore. When they came out of the water, they were horrified to see their clothes were gone. Thankfully, there were lots of trees by the shore, so they were able to cover themselves with leaves to wear for the sprint to their wagons. When they arrived, peals of laughter could be heard throughout the camp.

This is not funny to the man this happened to, but to the rest of the wagon train this is a hilarious story. It happened late last night. Jonah heard a wild animal foraging around his wagon. He thought he would chase the culprit away before it discovered his bags of dried food. He intended to drive off the animal with a large stick. There was only one problem with his plan. The wild animal was a skunk. Poor Jonah. He and his wagon were banished to the end of the wagon train and will have to lag a few wagon lengths behind for about a week—or until the obnoxious smell goes away.

Jeremiah brought three sheep along with him on the trail. They were all pregnant. He wanted the wool and when the ewes had a lamb he planned to have lamb chops. One ewe was especially good at getting stuck in interesting places. Maybe it's mean to laugh at the misfortunes of a stupid sheep, but this sheep would get stuck in empty barrels, crates, between boulders—literally everywhere. Sometimes it took a while for the sheep to be rescued, but no sooner would she be freed from whatever imprisoned her, she would jump right back into the same trap. I watched her do that several times. No wonder the Bible says, All we like sheep have gone astray. God frees us from traps, and we leap back in. I am so thankful we have a kind, loving Shepherd Who is so patient with us.

There are more problems. Prairie dogs. They cover the landscape. Their holes have caused the crippling and deaths of so many animals. I saw James' horse limp slowly towards camp a week ago. It had stepped into a prairie dog's hole and injured its leg. I heard James tell his wife—they are in the wagon just behind ours—if the horse wasn't walking properly by morning, he would have to shoot it. The animal was shot. dragged behind the wagon until evening, carved up, and the meat shared. I told Lachlan it wouldn't be safe to eat if it was left to broil in the hot sun all day. Lachlan tried to warn folks, but they refused to listen. Several got sick from the tainted meat.

Another problem with dragging an animal is that coyotes, mountain lions, and wolves come out at night and follow the scent all the way to camp. Children are not allowed out of the wagons at dusk. One little guy managed to escape the confines of his wagon and was carried off by a cougar. Thankfully, the boy's Pa saw the cougar and was able to shoot it before it got too far with his son. The boy was dragged by his arm, so thankfully only suffered a broken arm. I can't imagine the nightmares that child will have.

This is another scary bear story. This bear was enormous, much bigger than the bear with the spoon. He could easily kill a man with one swipe of his massive paw. This gigantic grizzly came shuffling and sniffing around our wagon the other day.

I think it must have smelled the barrels of bacon. If it had taken a notion to do so, it could have shredded the canvas and the wagon. I'm glad Sadie listens when I tell her to hush. Thankfully, Lachlan had his rifle handy. The whole wagon train had another bear feast party with singing and dancing. Of course, I waltzed with Lachlan again. That night was the best part of the trip so far. I am also getting quite a bear skin collection.

Little Lance Carter carefully planned his escape. When his Ma and Pa were busy, this little four-year old decided to go off in search of berries and butterflies. He got so busy with his adventure, he didn't notice the wagons had moved on. It's sad, Ma. We have lost so many children to their desire to explore. They wander off, and we never see them again. Thankfully, Lance's story has a happy ending.

A Shoshone warrior rode into camp with a small boy tucked under his arm. The boy looked like he was having the time of his life, until he saw his Pa's face. I don't think that boy will wander off again.

Honestly, this journey has been such an emotional ride. One moment I am rejoicing and laughing and feeling like my heart will burst with joy. Moments later, I hear of a tragedy and feel like my heart is being crushed with anguish.

What happened later that night was the saddest of all. It should only be in people's nightmares. I can't write about it now. It's too painful. I'll tell you about it when I can.

I love you, Ma.

CHAPTER SEVEN

Morning came way too early. To make any headway they had to be moving the wagons out just after seven—but getting up at 4:00 am just seemed inhumane to Rose.

"Rose, are you getting up?"

"Soon—"

"Rose, I've made coffee. Are you getting up now?"

Rose mumbled something garbled as Lachlan called out,

"I'm off to collect the oxen. I'll be back soon. Come on, Sadie."

When Lachlan returned, Rose was nowhere to be seen. There was no smell of breakfast being made. His stomach grumbled as he called out, "ROSE!"

A very sleepy head peeked out the back of the wagon.

"Rose, we're moving out soon."

"I'm sorry. I'm so tired. I was up half the night with Widow Jennings."

"Why, Rose?"

"I'm sad her husband didn't get to see their beautiful baby son. He's a fine child."

"Widow Jennings had a baby? I didn't know she was expecting."

"It was sad, Lachlan. Widow Jennings cried when she saw the baby. She said he looked so much like his dad."

Lachlan shook his head as he kneeled down to put the wagon wheels back on the wagon.

"How will Widow Jennings make it on the trail?" Lachlan wondered aloud.

"I have an idea," Rose said hesitantly.

"You always have an idea," Lachlan laughed.

"This is a great idea."

"All your ideas are great."

"Widow Jennings is all alone. A few men are trying to help her, but they're busy looking after their own wagons and families."

"And—?"

"Well, I wonder if it would be okay with you if Widow Jennings and her baby stayed with us. There's an extra bed. I can help her look after her baby. I just don't see how she can survive on her own."

"Have you asked her what she thinks of this idea?"

"No, I thought I'd ask you first."

"Would that be too much for you, Rose?"

"I'd love to help her."

Lachlan laughed as he said, "I think if you could, you'd have the entire wagon train living with us."

Rose smiled at him. "Does that mean yes?"

"If God put this on your heart, and it will save their lives, then yes."

Rose's eyes brimmed with tears.

"You're a good man, Lachlan James Smith."

"And you are a mighty fine woman, Rose Caroline Murphy."

Rose blushed. Sometimes the way Lachlan looked at her made her feel like her heart was melting.

"I'll talk to her when we stop for lunch."

"Speaking of lunch, is there anything I could have for breakfast?"

"Oh Lachlan, I'm so sorry I didn't have breakfast out for you. I have some bannock, cheese, coffee, and two boiled goose eggs. How does that sound?"

"It sounds like a feast, Rose. Thank you."

Rose was too tired to eat. She sat by the fire, nursing a very hot coffee, trying very hard to wake up.

"Rose, you look so tired. Why don't you sleep this morning while we travel?"

Hours later, Rose awoke with a start. The wagon wasn't moving. How could it be dark already? Why didn't Lachlan wake her?

As soon as she put her head out the back of the wagon, Lachlan leaped to his feet to help her.

"How was your sleep?"

"I didn't mean to sleep the entire day."

"You looked exhausted. If you're going to assist women in labor, you need to be well rested."

"But—I'm supposed to be preparing your meals."

"I can look after myself."

"But you said you'd starve without a cook—"

Rose saw the mischievous look in Lachlan's eyes.

"You didn't really need a cook?"

"I'm mighty glad you're cooking for me."

"I'm off to see Widow Jennings. I think she needs us. That would be wonderful if she and her baby came to live with us."

A short time later, Rose came back to the campfire, sobbing uncontrollably. Lachlan couldn't help himself. He jumped up, put his arms around her, and drew her close to comfort her. Rose cried until she had no tears left.

"Lachlan, they're both dead."

"What?"

"Widow Jennings and her sweet baby boy are dead."

"What happened?"

Rose had a hard time speaking. She leaned against Lachlan's chest and heard his heart beating. Somehow, the sound calmed her. The sobs subsided.

"She bled heavily. I think she needed a doctor. I'm not a doctor. I did all I could, but I don't know how to keep a woman from dying."

Rose started crying again. Sadie put her head in Rose's lap and just looked at her with big, soulful eyes. Her eyes said, "It's okay, Rose. I'm sure you did all you could." Ruby seemed to sense something was wrong. She curled up in Rose's lap and purred like a kitten.

"Rose, you did your best. It's not your fault."

"I feel terrible, Lachlan. I wish I had stayed with her longer last night. Maybe if I'd been there, I could've helped her."

"It's not your fault, Rose."

"Her bed was covered in blood."

"If she was bleeding severely there's nothing you could have done for."

"It's my fault."

"Rose, even trained medical doctors have patients die. What happened to the baby?"

Rose could barely speak through the sobs.

"Widow Jennings—was nursing him—she must have—fallen asleep—and died—on top of him. The baby—suffocated."

"None of this is your fault, Rose."

"Lachlan, I want to go home."

Thursday, June 1, 1854

Dear Ma,
I have horrible news. It's what I told you should only be in people's nightmares. Such pain should not exist in the world. I assisted at a labor a few days ago. Widow Jennings had a beautiful baby boy. He looked so much like his father. I went to see her the next day, to see if she would like to come live with us, because a woman alone with a newborn would never survive on the trail. Lachlan supported the idea.

This is worse than any nightmare I've ever had. This is so hard to say. I was horrified to see that she had hemorrhaged to death. She must have lain on top of the baby when she died. I found them both.

It was beyond terrible. I am so thankful for Lachlan's encouragement. He helped me see it wasn't my fault. He made me see, even if I had been present, there was nothing I could have done for her.

Ma, I was grieved to see a mom and her baby lying dead in a grave. Widow Jennings looked like she was having a nap holding her sweet little boy. The men dug the hole deep so wild animals wouldn't dig them up. The womenfolk pretty much covered the bodies with flowers. It was the most heartbreaking experience I've ever had. I wish there was something I could have done to help her. Today, I desperately want to go home.

Quite a few folks are talking about turning around and going back. Captain Whittaker is not amused. He said we are safer if we stay together. He even called a few of the men talking about going back cowards. That didn't go over well. I guess we'll find out in the morning how many will carry on to Oregon.

Owen and Willow came for dinner. They are such a precious couple—such welcome guests. I don't know if I've told you that Owen is Lachlan's brother. He's ten years older and raised Lachlan since he was a boy, ever since their parents died of cholera. He's a fine man. He adores his wife—a beautiful Sioux Indian. It's a joy to see the deep respect Willow shows her husband. He cherishes her. Their marriage is the most amazing love story I have ever seen.

Last night was a night for dreams. As we sat around the campfire, enjoying the peacefulness of the night, Owen asked, "Why are you on the trail, Rose? What dreams has God put on your heart?" I saw Lachlan lean forward. His body language said he wanted to hear the answer to that question. Maybe he hoped my dreams had changed since we last spoke about them?

I told them I was a teacher in Independence, Missouri, teaching at an all-girl's school—that I loved it, and thought I would be a spinster and stay at the school forever. One day, someone told me about the plight of children in the West. There were no schools, and even in some places where there were schools, there were no available teachers. There were so many teachers wanting to stay in the big city there were extra teachers who had no work. I wasn't needed. There were so many who would love to take my place. I don't know exactly how it happened, but when I heard that children weren't being given a chance to learn, it was like God planted a seed in my heart, and the longing to go to Oregon grew. I wanted to teach these teacherless, uneducated children.

Lachlan said, "I'm sure you'd be a blessing wherever you are." Then he shared his dream. He hoped to find a good piece of land, build a home, raise cattle and crops, ask a godly woman to be his wife, and have a family. It was kind of strange, Ma. He looked at me right after he shared his dream. It was like he wanted to see my reaction. I merely smiled at him. He had the strangest expression on his face. Maybe I'm imagining it, but if I could read his thoughts he would have been saying, "I'd love to ask you to be my wife, but that wouldn't work, because your dream takes place in a town, and my dream is far from town. It's obvious our life goals and dreams collide and run off in opposite directions."

Do you think it's funny I'd even think that? Maybe he was thinking what a nice supper he had or something not at all related to me. I asked Owen what his dream is.

"Well, we have given up nearly everything for this dream. We had a beautiful home and a thriving carpentry business, but we knew God was calling us to another place. We sold or gave away almost everything we owned because of the dream God put in our hearts."

Ma, I'm telling you the details so you can see it all. Owen paused to take a swig of his coffee. The fire crackled as sparks flew towards heaven. The stars seemed to be pulsating with brilliant light. An animal on a nearby hill cried to God for his supper. The wind blew ever so softly through the trees. Owen took Willow's hand as he continued. "We hope to find a good piece of land and raise cattle. I want to build a warm, cozy home for my beautiful wife." He squeezed her hand and she smiled at him.

"It has to be a place with a good Southern exposure so the rooms will be full of light. I hope it will be filled with children." He looked lovingly at Willow and gently moved his hand to cover her round belly. "This little gaffer's going to have a puppy and a swing in a tree as soon as he can walk. He will be one of the most loved little boys who ever lived."

"How do you know the baby's a boy?" Lachlan asked.
"Oh, I just know."
Willow just smiled. She gently laid her hand on top of Owen's as she said, "I feel tired, my love. Please may we go?"
Owen got up immediately. He picked up the bison skin that had been covering his precious wife, and gently wrapped it around her shoulders. Owen picked up his wife to carry her as if she weighed nothing.
"Thank you for the delicious rabbit stew," Owen said.
Willow smiled at me—her favorite student. "Yes, thank you. Rose, you're getting to be a fine cook." She is mighty proud of me.
"I agree," Lachlan said. "I knew she was going to be a great cook, the moment I laid eyes on her." I blushed. I don't know why I blush so often around that man.
Owen made a funny comment. "Now Lachlan, that definitely wasn't your first thought when you saw Rose."
Lachlan laughed. "You're right, but it was a close second thought when God gave me the idea to invite Rose along as my cook."

Ma, I have to say, having a baby raccoon and his mother—my Sadie—has brought so much joy to what otherwise could have been monotonous days. Watching them play has made me laugh more than I can remember laughing. Children love to visit. When

I grieved about the loss of my friend and her baby son, my pets were beside me to comfort me. You had to see it to believe it. Sadie is so good at keeping critters away. We have not had a rat problem as others have had. If any come around Sadie kills them and leaves them as presents for me on my bed. She means well—Ruby is so cute. Now that she's eating solid foods, she has quite the routine before she can eat. I have a bowl of water for her to drink out of, but she uses it as her wash bowl. Everything gets washed. Thoroughly.

This morning, when the bugle blared—I can't say it played— ten oxen teams left the train and turned around towards Independence. The homesickness and the hardships were too much for those folks. They heard the trail gets even more treacherous after the half-way point and were scared off by the stories. We waved at them as they passed. One woman was crying. It was the death of so many dreams. They would be going back to nothing.

The captain called a meeting that morning. The sun was barely peeking over the hills when he told us these folk were called "go-backs" or "turn-arounds." He spat a huge wad of chewing tobacco out as he said it. It was like he was spewing these folks out of his mouth with the chunk of tobacco. It will be dangerous for them. I pray God protects them.

I love you, Ma.

Chapter Eight

"Rose you've been working mighty hard. May I make dinner for you?" That was an unexpected question.

"Lachlan, you've been working mighty hard too, and I'm supposed to be your cook."

"I know, Rose, but I'd like to do something for you. You've been taking such good care of me. Your cooking is getting so good."

Rose smiled. Lachlan had such a kind heart. It was too bad his cooking skills weren't as good as his intentions. Rose ate the burned trout gratefully.

The wagon train was stopped to allow people a chance to bathe and hunt for the day. This would also be a cooking lesson day. Today Rose was going to learn to make bannock. Willow had been sending over baskets of it, but Rose had to learn to make it on her own.

Rose loved Willow more each day. Her quiet, gentle spirit was so soothing. There was a purity and innocence she saw in her friend. Rose wanted to keep this friend forever, but there was a problem. Willow wasn't a believer in the living God.

Perhaps God had more plans than just bannock. Maybe He wanted Willow to know about the bread of life.

God, please give me wisdom to speak your Words of life and truth to Willow.

"Willow, thank you for helping me learn to cook. I appreciate your kindness."

"You're welcome, Rose. I'm glad to have such an eager student who learns so quickly."

"I'm learning quickly because you're a great teacher."

As they kneaded the dough, Willow suddenly asked, "Rose, why are you so different from most other people I've met?"

"What do you mean?"

"There are people who seem to hate me because I'm an Indian."

"That means nothing to me. I only see you as a precious woman."

"Rose, I feel only love and acceptance from you."

"Willow, it must be because the Spirit of the living God lives in me."

"The living God? I don't know what you mean."

"Willow, what do you know about God?"

"Not much."

"What have you heard?"

"I've heard there is a God who loves all people."

"That is truth. He loves you, Willow."

"Why do you say that?"

"He loves you with an everlasting love. It says so in His Word. He has known you since before you were formed in your mother's womb."

"He has known me before birth?"

"Yes, Psalm 139 explains this so well. May I read it to you?"

Willow nodded as she continued kneading.

"O Lord, You have searched me and known me. You know when I sit down and when I rise up; You discern my thoughts from afar. You search out my path and my lying down and are acquainted with all my ways. Even before a word is on my tongue, behold, O Lord, You know it altogether.

You hem me in, behind and before, and lay Your hand upon me. Such knowledge is too wonderful for me; it is high; I cannot attain it. Where shall I go from your Spirit? Or where shall I flee from your Presence?

If I ascend to heaven, You are there! If I make my bed in Sheol, You are there! If I take the wings of the morning and dwell in the uttermost parts of the sea, even there Your hand shall lead me, If I say, "Surely the darkness shall cover me, and the light about me be night," even the darkness is not dark to you; the night is bright as the day, for darkness is as light with you.

For You formed my inward parts; You knitted me together in my mother's womb. I praise you, for I am fearfully. And wonderfully made. Wonderful are Your works; my soul knows it very well.

My frame was not hidden from You, when I was being made in secret, intricately woven in the depths of the earth. Your eyes saw my unformed substance, in Your book were written, every one of them, the days that were formed for me, when as yet there was none of them.

How precious to me are Your thoughts, O God! How vast is the sum of them! If I would count them, they are more than the sand. I awake, and I am still with You."

"How do I know this is true?"

"The Bible, God's Word, tells us He spoke the Universe into being. He is all powerful. He numbers the stars and calls them by name. He knows how many hairs are on your head. He knows the thoughts you think."

"Amazing."

"It's truly amazing. The Bible says, 'In Him we live and move and have our being.' Without Him we would not take our next breath."

"Incredible."

"Willow, the God who created the Heavens and the Earth loves you. You are precious to Him."

"But how do I know this is true?"

"Ask Him to reveal Himself to you, Willow. Ask Him to show you He is God. He loves you with an everlasting love. You can trust Him."

"How do I find Him?"

"The Bible says if you seek Him, you will find Him, if you search for Him with all your heart."

"If He created me and loves me, and knows everything about me, I want to know Him."

"Willow, may I pray to God with you?"

"I would like that."

"Dear Father in Heaven, thank You for Your amazing love. Thank You that You have seen and known Willow since before she was born. Thank you that You didn't let her die when she was a baby. You brought people to find her and gave her a family to love and care for her. Thank You that You have given her a husband who adores her. Thank you, she is precious to You. Please help her find You."

"Thank you, Rose."

Monday, June 12, 1854

Dear Ma,

We arrived near Fort Bridger, Wyoming, on the Green River late last night. Ma, it's so beautiful here. The smell of sage and prairie roses is thick in the air. The sunsets are spectacular. The sky bursts with color. It's very hard on the trail, yet there are many moments that are so awesome they take your breath away. The tall prairie grasses seem to whisper "Be at peace, My child. I am with you."

We've traveled over three hundred miles from Fort Laramie. Captain Whittaker wants to be sure we are over the Rockies before snowfall, and he says at this rate we'll be fine.

We plan to visit the fort in the morning. I heard the post was established around 1842 by Jim Bridger, a mountain man, so it was named after him. It's a huge supply fort, so people are looking forward to stocking up on vegetables and gunpowder. We've been traveling for over two months now, so provisions are getting low.

We had Captain Whittaker at our campfire for dinner last night. It takes him almost two months to visit each wagon for a meal. He said it's his way of keeping his finger on the pulse of his wagon train. I think it's also to get in on the great cooking that can be smelled from all the campfires. I think he's lonely and appreciates the company. Sadie seems very suspicious of him. She sits by me, staring at him, keeping her distance from the captain. Maybe the smell of tobacco reminds her of the prospector who was going to shoot her.

We haven't seen Fort Bridger yet, but the captain described it to us. He said the fort is kind of wild looking. I can't imagine what he means, because most of what we see on the trail is wild looking. He said there's an eight-foot-high log fence with pointed tops around the stockade. There are four small log cabins with sod roofs in the middle of the enclosure. That sounds a lot smaller than I expected for a major stopping spot for on the trail. He told us one of the cabins is the black-smith forge and carpenter shop, another cabin is the general store, and the other two cabins are residences. He plans to have the wagons stay at the fort for two days. Folks will be happy to hear there's a blacksmith shop, because some folks need to get the iron rims on their wagon wheels fixed before they roll off.

We had another wedding the other day. It's surprising how many romances are springing up. It's also surprising such young women are being allowed to marry. I'm twenty-one, Ma, and I don't feel ready for marriage. The bride was only seventeen. Maybe folks feel life is so uncertain why waste time waiting? A great thing about these marriages is the rejoicing and celebrating that goes on. It's wonderful to behold. It's a good chance for people to forget all the hardships of the trail, at least for a few hours.

Several babies have been born in the last two months. I thank God most have survived so far. I'm finding being a doula is keeping me quite busy. I'm thankful God has me here, otherwise these women would be on their own with no one to help them. Many of the women I've helped have offered to pay me, but even though I said I don't want anything, provisions mysteriously appear in our wagon. Sometimes there's a thank you note attached. Sometimes it's anonymous. Even though it's unexpected, it gives us more to share with others.

People seem to love coming to our campfire in the evenings. I think there's a few families who are still in this wagon train because of Lachlan. He has the gift of encouragement. I don't think anyone could be depressed around him if they tried.

I almost hate to tell you this story, but I'm trying to show you what life is like here. A three-year old boy went off exploring and didn't hear his wagon pulling out. His Ma assumed the little guy was riding with his dad. His Pa assumed he was in the wagon with his mother. He wasn't discovered missing until nightfall. His Pa and a handful of men spent half the night retracing our wagon tracks trying to find the boy. They never did find out if he had fallen prey to wild animals, or as some suspected, had been carried off by Indians. I find that last part hard to believe. If he was found I believe the Indians would have made every effort to bring him back to us.

I've heard most of the Indians are peaceful, which is a blessing because Fort Bridger is completely surrounded by several large nations. The Shoshone and Bannock Indians have helped us with scouting. I heard they've provided food to wagon trains when folks were running out of provisions. Many a bison was dragged into a pioneer camp by Indian warriors and left for starving travelers. Several Indians made ferries out of their canoes and used them to pull wagons and take people across treacherous rivers. They didn't need to do that. They were definitely being good Samaritans. I don't understand why people are spreading such terrible stories about them.

This next issue makes me mad. This has happened at every fort we've been to. Indian hunters bring their merchandise, mostly fox and beaver pelt, but sometimes buffalo hides and *beautiful beaded moccasins, to trade at the forts with settlers and merchants. This is the problem—which is in violation of federal law. The Indians are paid with alcohol and trinkets—handfuls of beads. Sadly, the Indian warriors love the taste of whiskey, so they trade their valuable furs for a bottle. It's so unfair.*

You may have heard gruesome stories of massacres from Indians on the warpath, but as far as I can see, the Indians are peaceful. You probably have not heard their side. I've heard terrible stories of trigger-happy pioneers shooting at friendly Indians for target practice. Who would do such a thing? Maybe the pioneers heard of Indian attacks and hoped to scare them away by shooting first. But that is no excuse. Maybe that's why Indians have attacked wagon trains—for revenge for what happened to their people. There's really no law out here, Ma. It seems people are doing whatever is right in their own eyes. This really is the Wild West. Did I mention I'd like to go home?

Dysentery has swept through the train. People have high fevers, bloody stools, and are vomiting. Captain Whittaker just rode his horse down the row of wagons tonight shouting to everyone we are no longer staying at Fort Bridger for two days. We are moving out in the morning. We will not be waiting for wheels to be fixed. When the merchant at the fort discovered we have dysentery—I'm not sure how he found out—he told our captain the fort gates will remain locked. He won't allow us to enter in the morning. The disease is highly infectious. I don't blame him for locking his gates. Dysentery can kill a person in a few days. It's too bad, though, because there went all hopes for new wagon wheels and fresh vegetables. Thankfully, Lachlan and I are well. We've been able to bring meals to those who are sick.

We are presently locked outside the gates waiting for morning so we can move on. Fires can be seen in the distance from the Indian's camps. They are that close. Hopefully they leave us alone. We mean them no harm.

The barrels of bacon we bought back in Independence have gone rancid. The barrels were covered in tar to keep them airtight and the bacon was stored in sawdust, but obviously that didn't help.

We aren't sure if the water of the Green River is safe to drink. We saw a dead beaver floating on it. If we don't replenish our water barrels soon, people will die of dehydration, so we really have no choice but to use that water. Men have taken huge barrels to the river to fill. Some of the menfolk went fishing. A few trout were caught, but not enough to share.

Have I told you about the hunting expeditions? There have been days we've camped to allow the men to hunt for fresh meat. It's very abundant here. We've had ducks, geese, rabbit, quail, antelope, bison, elk, deer, moose, and bear. We've found lots of wild berries. God has prepared a table before us in the presence of our enemies—disease and wild creatures.

Folks tied cages filled with chickens to their wagons, hoping for eggs along the way, but the birds are too nervous to lay eggs. I guess being jostled and bumped for hours every day would be scary for a chicken. Half my recipes don't work without eggs. There have been a few times I've come across quail or goose eggs while looking for herbs and fuel. Have you seen how tiny quail eggs are? At least they are better than nothing.

A number of women and I spent the afternoon collecting fuel for fires. We use anything we can find that looks like it will burn: sagebrush, dead trees, dried buffalo manure 'chips', willow branches, and any other bits of wood we can find. There's no point cutting a tree and trying to use it for firewood. If the wood is green the fire will just smoke and won't burn.

Lachlan strikes a flint against steel to get a spark for a fire. He also brought matches in watertight containers, but with my terrible fire-building skills, they were used up long ago. If someone has a fire going, folks often bring a piece of wood, start it on fire, then carry the burning firebrand to use it to start their own fire.

Cooking over an open fire was something I've definitely had to get used to. The main cooking items we have are a large Dutch oven pot and a cast iron frypan. We have a collection of things that come in mighty handy—a sharp butcher knife, several large wooden spoons, and a soup ladle. There's a coffee pot and a metal tripod contraption that has three legs that holds the pot over the fire.

Lachlan has an assortment of cow stomach flasks and canvas bags for collecting water. Collecting water is something I've discovered I love. We've camped by such spectacular scenery, by so many beautiful rivers and streams, it's been a joy to collect water and see all the beauty. Lachlan and I love to walk together. He carries his rifle and walks with me to protect me.

I had the honor of telling Willow about God. I pray she opens her heart to Him.

I love you, Ma.

Chapter Nine

Rose awoke to the sound of screaming. It was the middle of the night. Her first thought was she must help whoever sounded so desperate. Jumping out of the back of the wagon without Lachlan's hand wasn't as easy as she anticipated. She slept so soundly she didn't realize there had been a terrible thunderstorm. This wasn't just any rain. It had been a torrential downpour. The lovely lace-up leather boots were not designed for slippery mud. Rose landed with a thud in a puddle. Her beautiful boots and designer lace petticoat were covered in mud.

She didn't mean to cry out, but the puddles and mud were so unexpected, Rose let out a scream. Sadie woke up startled and started barking. Ruby woke up screaming. Lachlan heard the commotion and got up to see what was going on. Rose looked ready to cry. The look on her face was, "Why on earth did I ever come here?"

Lachlan took one look at Rose sprawled in the mud and burst out laughing. The humor of the situation finally got to her, and Lachlan's laugh was so infectious, she laughed too.

"Sorry for laughing, Rose, but you look a sight, plunked right in the mud, wearing the most beautiful dress I've ever seen." Lachlan reached out a hand to help her up.

Rose was about to make a snappy remark—something about her being just fine—that she had the situation entirely under control and didn't require any assistance—but she didn't say anything. It was obvious she really did need him.

The ground oozed mud. Everywhere. With a mischievous twinkle in her eyes, Rose grabbed hold of that strong hand and pulled with all her might. She couldn't help it. He asked for it. Lachlan fell onto his hands and knees in the mud. They probably would have had a splendid mud fight right then and there, but a piercing scream caught their attention.

Who could it be? She held Lachlan's arm so there would be no more repeat falls as they hurried in the direction of the sound. It was only moments, but it seemed she held his arm for an eternity. The butterflies in her stomach were having a party.

Both were surprised to hear the cries came from Owen and Willow's wagon. It couldn't be the baby. It was too soon. Way too soon.

"Hello," Lachlan called. "Is everything okay?"

A head appeared out the back of the wagon. Owen looked frantic. His eyes were wild, his sandy hair a disheveled mess.

"Oh, thank God you're here. I don't know what to do. Willow has gone into labor. But it's too early—"

"May I climb into the wagon?" Rose asked.

"Of course. I was praying you'd come."

Owen jumped down as Lachlan helped Rose climb up.

"Thank you, Rose, for helping us," Owen said. "Much obliged to you."

"Lachlan, the wagon train will be pulling out soon," Rose whispered. "The captain isn't going to wait. Pray the baby comes quickly."

Lachlan wanted to ask Owen to pray with him, but it was obvious there was no point. He seemed unaware of anything but his wife's agonizing screams. His brother was completely oblivious to the muddy mess of his helpers and anything else around him.

"Lachlan, boil some water. Bring me clean cloths. Hurry."

"Yes, ma'am."

Rose poured water over her hands to get the mud off. She found a soft cloth and dipped it in water in the washstand bowl—placing the cooled cloth on Willow's forehead.

"Shhhh. It's okay, Willow. You'll be fine."

Willow looked at Rose and smiled, just before her face contorted and she let out another horrific scream.

"It's okay, Willow. You'll be fine. Shhhhh."

Rose continued wiping the perspiration off her friend's face until Lachlan returned. Rose reached through the flap for the cloths. When she reached for the pail of boiling water, Lachlan said, "I'll carry it up for you." Rose didn't argue.

Once in the wagon, Lachlan held both of Rose's hands in his and prayed.

"Father God, we humbly come before you on behalf of Willow, the baby, and Rose. Please be with them. May Willow have strength to deliver. Please help Rose be brave and strong."

Lachlan squeezed Rose's hands, then climbed out of the wagon to sit at the campfire with his brother.

"Rose, thank you for coming." The voice was so weak, Rose barely recognized it. The woman lying on the crude wooden bed looked so pale and tired. Her usually silky dark hair was tangled, her eyes looked at the world through a haze of pain. There was no color in her face at all.

"I'm glad to be here for you and your baby," she said aloud, but under her breath she whispered, "Dear God, please don't let Willow die."

Owen and Lachlan paced anxiously for hours outside the wagon. An anguished look crossed his face when Owen heard the bugle.

"We don't have much time now."

"It's okay. God will look after us," Lachlan said.

"But what if the wagons leave without us?"

"Don't worry, Owen. We'll catch up."

"Maybe you should keep going. I'll catch up."

"I'm not leaving you."

"Are you sure?"

"I can't leave without my cook, and you couldn't possibly travel alone. It would be too dangerous."

The look in Owen's eyes was heartbreaking. He knew if they stayed behind, it risked death for them all. He also knew childbirth in a bumpy wagon could be agonizing or death for Willow and the baby.

Heaving himself up on the wagon, Owen called to Willow from the doorway. He didn't know how to handle this situation. He trusted Willow's advice. "Willow, the wagon train has to pull out soon. Will you be okay if we pull out?"

Owen was surprised to hear Rose reply, "That'll be fine."

"Why didn't Willow answer?'

"She's too weak. Pray for us."

The worry in Owen's eyes turned to fear.

"Is she going to be okay, Rose?"

"I don't know. Pray."

The men separated to collect their oxen and their wagon wheels from the river. Lachlan tethered his stallion to the back of his wagon.

Owen attached the wheels as he prayed fervently for his wife and unborn child. "Dear Lord, please spare their lives."

Thursday, June 22, 1854

Dear Ma,

Last night was the best night and the worst night of my life. I was a midwife again. It was an honor to be with Willow as she brought her baby son into the world. I did everything I could. I cut his cord with a sterilized knife and tied it securely, I cleaned him with warm water, I wrapped him snugly in clean cloths.

I did everything I could, Ma. He wouldn't nurse. He was not ready to be born. He came way too early. We watched him slowly turn blue and then leave this life. It was so sad. Willow didn't cry. She held her baby son close and sang to him. Maybe she hoped she could call his spirit back.

When the wagons stopped for the noon meal, it was with the most profound grief I opened the tarp flap and told Owen he had a baby son who was now with God. It was so hard to see his face transform from joy to grief. He wanted to know if Willow lived. I assured him she was fine. Lachlan grabbed his brother and held him as he sobbed with relief for his wife and grief for his son.

By the time we stopped for the night, Willow's face was flushed and her forehead was burning hot. I must have startled the men when I screamed out the back flap, "Pray!" I put cool cloths on Willow's head well into the night. I prayed the whole time, "Dear God, please don't take Willow now. It would kill Owen. He can't lose both his beautiful wife and his precious baby son. Please God."

Thankfully, He heard me. The fever broke around midnight. I gave Willow water to drink, then wearily tried to climb out of the wagon. I must have fainted, because the next thing I remember I was on the little bed in our wagon. Lachlan held a cold cloth on my forehead and covered me with a blanket. I looked at him for an explanation, but he just shushed me and told me to rest. It's the middle of the night. I'm wide awake now with nothing to do but talk with God and write to you.

Have I ever told you about a typical day, Ma? Today was not a typical day. Usually everyone wakes up at four in the morning to the blast of the bugle. Breakfast is made by the women folk while the men collect the grazing animals and the wagon wheels. Today it seemed like the whole world was tired. I couldn't get up. I had orders to sleep.

The Pawnee and Shoshone trail guides usually arrive around seven o'clock most mornings. Today they didn't come because we are staying in camp for the day. On all other days, a group of men—the wagon train's scouts—ride ahead with the Indians to scout the path. As soon as they return, Captain Whittaker sounds the bugle and shouts, "Wagons Ho!"

We always stop at noon for an hour to water the animals, to eat, drink, and rest. By one pm we head back out on the trail. Around five pm—or whenever we find a suitable campsite with water and grass for the animals—we set up camp for the night.

By seven pm, the womenfolk clean up and do any chores necessary before bed. Sometimes in the evenings, friends visit. There might be musical instruments, singing, stories, and dancing. Usually by eight pm everyone settles in for the night. The men take turns being on guard duty to protect the camp. Half the men patrol from eight until midnight. At midnight the guard changes.

I can't believe I slept till noon today. I made a pile of Johnnycakes and took some over to Owen and Willow for their lunch. It was the first time I saw my friend cry. She was still holding her dead baby, crying softly, as she realized he was really gone. Her face looked grieved. Owen tried to persuade her to give him their son so he could be buried. The thought was obviously way too painful. She couldn't hand him over.

When I brought supper over around six pm—venison sage stew—Willow was still holding her child. Her husband insisted she hand him the baby. He said it wasn't healthy to hold on to a dead child. She reluctantly handed her baby over. The finality of his death must have hit her, because that's when she started to wail. It was dreadful. I pray God comforts them both.

Did you notice I seldom mention baths? That's because they happen so rarely, only when we are camped near a river or lake. Bath days are also clothes washing days, hunting days, and wedding days. I know I mentioned it before, but it's so surprising how many romances have sprung up along the way. Last week we had four weddings on bath day. I'm *surprised there are that many unattached people on this wagon train.*

I don't think I told you I made a good friend. Jane is from New York and is one of the sweetest girls I have ever met. She's about my age and was also a teacher. Jane came along as a governess for Luke, as his wife died, leaving him with two small children. Well, to no one's surprise, they fell in love. Jane asked me to be her maid of honor.

We had so much fun preparing for her wedding. I loaned her my hand-made white lace gown, the one you embroidered for me. It fit her perfectly. We spent the morning bathing, laughing, and searching for wildflowers for her hair. That was pretty easy as they cover the land as far as you can see. We found pink wild roses and made a garland with them. Jane looked radiant with the gorgeous dress and the halo of flowers adorning her waist-long, wavy blonde hair.

I watched four men on horse-back hauling a huge buffalo by the legs. This animal was to be roasted at several fires for today's wedding feast. The women each brought a cake to German Oma's wagon. She is known as one of the best cooks on the trail. She stacked the cakes with her delicious apple butter between them and covered the top with roses to make a stunning tiered wedding cake. It's called Molasses Stack Cake and it's expensive to make so it's only used for very special occasions.

Luke asked Lachlan to stand with him as his best man. I have never seen Lachlan look handsomer. A preacher performed the wedding. He's quite busy on this wagon train, looking after funerals, weddings, and Sunday meetings.

My friend Jane had every intention of being a school teacher out west, just like me, but it was obvious from her vows she had found an even greater love than teaching. Her beautiful vows were from Ruth 1:16 to 17.

"But Ruth replied, "Don't urge me to leave you or to turn back from you. Where you go, I will go, and where you stay, I will stay. Your people will be my people, and your God my God. Where you die, I will die, and there I will be buried. May the Lord deal with me, be it ever so severely, if even death separates you and me."

Luke's gaze at his beloved was heart melting. He said his verses were from the Song of Solomon. I've never heard a man speak more earnestly as Luke did when he took Jane's hands, gazed into her eyes, and said, "Set me as a seal upon thine heart, as a seal upon thine arm: for love is strong as death: jealousy is as cruel as the grave: the coals thereof are coals of fire, which hath a most vehement flame. You are my beloved. I will love you and cherish you all the days God gives us."

The vows were so beautiful the bride, the groom, and the guests cried. Strangely, those were the same verses Lachlan and I read to each other when we sat by the fire on our first night on the trail.

That's all for now. I'm praying you and the girls are well. I miss you.

I love you, Ma.

Chapter Ten

"Rose, you need to keep your fishing line in the water if you hope to catch anything."

"I'm trying, but I can't quite get the hang of it."

"That's cause you're a girl." Lachlan laughed at his own joke.

Not quite sure if she should ignore that comment, or throw something at him, Rose chose to laugh. He was right. Fishing was not for her.

"This oasis sure is beautiful."

"You're right, Lachlan. I've seen so much beauty on this trail I never knew existed."

"Me too, Rose."

Why is he smiling at me like that?

Sunday, June 25, 1854

Dear Ma,

This was such a restful day. Because it's Sunday, we didn't travel. It was so hot, when we laid the wash out on the grass, it dried in no time at all. After we finished our chores, Lachlan tried to teach me to fish. Even though the river seemed full of fish, and everyone else seemed to catch them easily, I couldn't catch a thing. Even Sadie jumped in and caught a fish. She gave it to her Ruby who washed it thoroughly, sat down on the grass, chuckling at her lunch. I confess I am hopeless at fishing. Thankfully, Lachlan filled a bucket with fine trout, so we were able to have Owen and Willow over for a fish fry. We are all trying to cheer Willow up. I can't imagine how sad it would be to lose a baby.

We've traveled over three hundred miles since we left Fort Laramie. We are by the Sweetwater River in Wyoming, camped near a giant granite outcropping that Lachlan told me is over one hundred and twenty feet high. It's huge. Folks call it Independence Rock. He said it was called that because fur trappers camped and celebrated Independence Day there in 1830. For over twenty years, pioneers have visited that rock and carved their names and the dates they visited. Some even wrote where they came from and where they're headed.

Lachlan went to see it alone. I couldn't go. I was too busy trying to get a fire going—wasting a pile of matches Lachlan traded for his wooden spoons—and trying to make dinner. By the time I finished it was dark. There was really no point to go. When Lachlan returned, he told me he saw thousands of pioneer's names carved into the rock. Captain Whittaker told us this is the half-way point of the journey. People wanted to sign their names to tell others they were alive and had made it safely that far.

During dinner I found this part of the conversation difficult to understand. Owen had a strange look on his face when he said, "Lachlan, Willow and I went for a stroll earlier today. The view of Independence Rock is amazing. It's so huge up close." He looked at Lachlan as if he expected him to understand what he was saying. Lachlan seemed confused.

Owen looked at his brother and smiled. It was a knowing smile. "There are so many names carved in that rock. It's like a giant guest book in the desert." Lachlan suddenly seemed to understand what his brother was hinting about, and his face turned beet red. It made me wonder what that was all about. There was obviously a secret. Maybe Lachlan will tell me one day?

We left Independence Rock this morning and have been climbing the foothills of the Rocky Mountains towards the

South Pass. I didn't expect the land to change so suddenly. It seemed like we blinked and found ourselves translated from a forest into a desert.

The next day, we traveled to a breathtakingly gorgeous place the captain told us is called Thomas Fork. The mountains on either side of the plain surrounded us. Thick stands of fir trees cascaded down the sides of the mountains. It was a bit unnerving to see snow on the tops of the mountains. I didn't expect to see snow in June.

Crossing clear streams, we went through lush green valleys and saw many stands of poplar and birch. We came to a place that was so steep, I wasn't sure if the wagons would make it. I could hardly keep myself seated as we climbed steep hills and descended into deep valleys. Some of the hills were so treacherous, even the animals mutinied. Prodding the lead oxen to coerce them to carry on, several men had to fight with their animals to get them to continue on the trail. Some oxen absolutely refused to go any further and had to be left behind.

When we came to a fork in the Bear River, we were surprised to meet up with men who said we must pay one dollar for each wagon to cross their toll bridge. Some grumbled about this, but after looking at the raging river, most decided one dollar wasn't that bad a price. Their lives were worth more than a dollar.

After dinner, we were surprised when Jonah, one of the night watchmen, rode down the wagon train. He informed everyone something spooked our horses and they stampeded. They were gone. Jonah was a godly man, and advised any who had the notion to pray, to kindly ask God for a miracle. He said he couldn't tell in the darkness where the animals went and it was pointless to chase after them at night. He said at morning light we would have to add searching for renegade horses to our list of chores.

The next morning, for some reason that couldn't be explained except for God's intervention, the horses were all back grazing with the oxen. Lachlan's stallion is so precious to him. I can't imagine the loss he would feel if it ran off.

Ma, I'm sorry many of these stories are hard to hear, but I'd be lying to you if I only presented a rosy picture. When a new mother dies, which happens too often, and the baby lives, the child is given to another nursing mother. Many of the mothers gave their babies cow's milk. They thought that would be richer and healthier for the baby. Unfortunately, if a cow had been grazing on white snakeroot or poison ivy, the milk would be toxic. Many of our babies died from the deadly milk. We didn't know what caused the deaths until a doctor in the next fort told us not to give our babies cow's milk.

I just experienced the most unusual week of my life. A man who was traveling alone showed up at our campfire wondering if he could join our wagon train for safety. He said his name was Running Bear, and he belonged to the Shoshone nation. He was running for his life. Sadie immediately befriended him.

He told us his axe head had flown off while he chopped wood, killing his friend Flying Eagle instantly. He said it was an accident—he was innocent—and I believe him. He said there was an avenger of blood, a relative of the dead man, who would be on his trail, seeking to kill him. Maybe Running Bear thought California or Oregon would be a safe place to hide? He said he had to get away. I'm not sure exactly how he conveyed all that to us as his English was very broken.

Running Bear ate my venison stew like he hadn't eaten for days. When the bowl was empty his eyes begged for more so I filled it twice. He was kind enough to give Ruby a piece of potato from the stew. He must never have seen a raccoon *washing her food as he watched her, seemingly fascinated by her cleaning her potato.*

When he seemed comfortable with us he took off his hat. I was so surprised. I have never seen a man with long hair like women's hair. It was braided and longer than mine. The beaded leather straps securing the braid were exquisitely woven.

This is where the story gets crazy. Running Bear spoke to us about God. He said God knew of his innocence, so he asked Him to lead and be his guide. He felt led to follow the wagon trails. When our wagon train appeared, he hid behind some thick trees and waited for God to show him which wagon would accept him. He knew he had to be cautious. He had heard of white men shooting Indians for sport. Being all alone made him very vulnerable. As he watched the wagons pass, Running Bear became confused. Maybe this wasn't God's plan after all? Almost all the wagons had passed, and he had no sign from God which wagon was a place of safety. He was almost ready to ride away, when he saw our wagon. He said it glowed as if it was on fire.

The Shoshone believe God leads them by dreams and visions. He felt the wagon on fire was a sign from God that we were good people. He followed at a distance, then came to our campfire under the cover of darkness. He believed God showed him we would protect him. He was right. Lachlan spoke to the captain, asking permission for our guest to travel with us under our care. Even though the man was penniless, Captain Whittaker agreed he could stay if he would be of assistance to the widows. He could put their wagon wheels in the water at night and put the wheels back on in the mornings. Running Bear was so grateful to be allowed to stay with us. He slept by Lachlan under the wagon.

Running Bear told us so many interesting things about his people we would never have known. In the summer they live in something called teepees. Poles are joined at the top to make a cone shape. Buffalo hides cover them. They can be easily taken down and transported while the tribe follows the buffalo. He said his nation are also called, 'The Sage Grass House People,' because when it's colder they cover their teepees with grasses.

Our guest was surprised to meet Willow. He stood and spoke to her in his native tongue, assuming she understood, not knowing she had white parents. Willow shyly told him she only spoke English. He told us he had a wife who looked after his five children—a beautiful woman like Willow. His wife gathered plants for food, butchered and cooked the bison, did household chores, and made clothing for the family. His face looked sad when he spoke of his family. He thought they would be so ashamed of him. He was grieved he would never have the opportunity to tell them of his innocence. He cried, then apologized, and told us men must be brave and not cry. Lachlan told him that was nonsense. All men with hearts cry.

Our friend told us the men of his tribe hunt, fight battles, fish, make spears and arrows, and look after the decisions for the family and the tribe. The chief is thought to have supernatural powers. There are two warrior groups, the Yellow Brows who are the young warriors, and the Logs, the older men. He told us the men hunt elk, deer, moose, jackrabbits, beaver, and mountain sheep.

It's a blessing to have another man to help around the wagon train. Because he's our friend, no one dares mistreat him. No one wants to see if Lachlan or Owen has a temper. They don't, but I won't tell anyone. I'll leave them guessing.

I am sorry to relate this part of our journey to you. It illustrates how fragile life is—not just here on the Oregon Trail—but for all of us.

Running Bear took the widows wagon wheel rims to the river for the night. He didn't return for dinner. Lachlan and Owen took torches to the river in search of our friend. Sadie went with them. Our friend lay face down by the bank of the river, with a feathered arrow in his back. Lachlan said Sadie howled mournfully and got all the coyotes mourning with her. We only knew him for a week, but it was an honor to meet such a fine man. The men buried him where he fell. May his soul rest in peace.

A precious black woman named Jemimah told me she had been born into slavery. Her grandparents had been brought over to the colonies from the Congo on a slave ship. Her master in South Carolina had left a will saying upon his death, all his slaves were to be freed. Jemimah didn't know what to do with herself when she was told she was free to leave. She didn't know what freedom looked like. Jemimah told us,

"My massa, he's a fine man. Ain't no kinder man dan him in the whole world. He gave me ma freedom."

I asked Jemimah what it was like as a slave.

"I was on a plantation. I worked sun up 'til sun down pickin' cotton and doin' chores, Missy. My massa gave his slaves wages. I's given a sack o' gourd seed meal, a sack o' cornmeal, and half a pound o' bacon once a week. That's all my food, Missy."

"It must have been hard, Jemimah."

"Missy, I ain't complainin', my massa a good man—he freed me—but I ain't goin' back to that life. I lived in a small shack by the swamps. Them mosquitos was thick. It was a hard life, Missy."

Ma, I'm telling you the details so you can see it all. Jemimah told me she found work with the Pringles family and was their helper on the trail. Their agreement was, at the end of the trail, Jemimah would be free to go wherever she liked.

Ma, I have grown to love this dear woman. She has assisted me at several births and helped me go on when I thought I couldn't. She's been a gift from God. I know Captain Whittaker will vouch for the fact that she's a free woman. He saw her papers before we started the trip.

I love you, Ma.

Chapter Eleven

"Rose, would you like to walk along the river with me?"

"I'd love to."

They walked in silence, breathing in the beauty surrounding them. The river was sparkling clear. It sang as it cascaded over the boulders. The sky was turning from deep blue into a glorious crimson sunset. Night sounds started ever so slowly. An owl flew overhead in search of fat prairie gophers. The air seemed filled with a deep contentment—like God was smiling on His creation. Sadie walked along beside Rose. Ruby scampered at their heels.

Rose had the thought if she stumbled over the boulders by the river, Lachlan would reach out and steady her. But that seemed manipulative, so she decided against it. Almost as soon as she decided it was a silly idea, she stumbled and Lachlan reached out and held her arm to steady her. She felt so protected and safe. They continued to walk in silence, with her arm still being held, until Lachlan spoke.

"When's your birthday, Rose?"

"It's funny you ask."

"Why?"

"Because it's tomorrow."

"That's odd. I was wondering all morning about your birthday."

"Why?"

"I don't know. July 21st seems like a great day for a birthday."

"I can't believe I'll be twenty-two."

"You're still young, Rose. You aren't officially an old maid until you are twenty-three."

"Very funny."

"Rose, it seems like you've been deep in thought all day. What have you been thinking about?"

"Oh, not much."

"Rose?"

"I've been thinking how short a time we have on Earth—how quickly time passes. It seems like a few heartbeats ago I was a little girl in an orphanage. I blinked and I was with the Murphys. My teacher's training and two years of teaching seem like they were but a moment. I blinked again,

and I was on a wagon on the Oregon Trail with you. Now I'm nearly twenty-two."

"I know what you mean, Rose. The Bible says our lives are a vapor."

Why, you do not even know what will happen tomorrow. What is your life? You are a mist that appears for a little while and then vanishes.

"James 4:14 is so true. I wonder what God has planned for my little mist of a life? I pray whatever it is, that it brings joy to His heart, honors Him, and brings Him glory."

"I'm sure it will, Rose. What are your plans for your birthday?"

"Well, because it's wash day, I imagine that will take most of my day. Captain Whittaker said there's a lovely deep swimming hole at Soda Springs. I'm so glad the Murphys taught me to swim. At least I don't have to worry about drowning."

Thursday, July 20, 1854

Dear Ma,

I know this won't surprise you—so many of my stories have been pretty crazy—so this story will fit right in with the rest. This happened in Snake River Canyon, Idaho.

There's a young man named Cyrus Parker who is traveling with his elderly Ma and Pa. They keep to themselves most of the time. Well, this story brings to mind your warning, "Watch out for snakes in the grass and snakes among men."

Every time Cyrus rode by my wagon, he would smile and say, "Howdy, ma'am". The only thing that's odd about that is he would pass by my wagon about half a dozen times in an hour. I felt so uncomfortable. He obviously was not riding to the end of the wagon train as he was supposed to. It seemed like he just rode for about five minutes then turned around. I wonder why he had no issues with the captain, as he obviously wasn't doing what he was supposed to. I guess the captain didn't know—

Also, this is so strange. When the women folk wash or sit around together to sew or visit, I have often seen Cyrus sitting fairly close by, staring at me. It's so creepy. I don't see other men sitting on hillsides or cliffs watching us. I try to sit with my back to him, so I don't have to look at him. Even then, I can feel his stare. He should be off doing chores with the menfolk.

I mentioned all this to Lachlan, and his face had an expression on it I've never seen before. I can't tell you exactly what the emotion was. Anger? Jealousy? Outrage? Maybe all of that. He never said a thing, but I could tell he wasn't pleased.

Well, a few days ago the womenfolk were out picking berries. I found an area that was full of ripe berries, so I stayed there while my friends moved on. I knew I could easily catch up with them. After about half an hour of picking, I suddenly had a strange feeling that I was being watched. It was unnerving. I wondered if a cougar was stalking me or if I encroached on a bear's berries. I realized with alarm I had lagged so far behind I was completely separated from the group. I was so far off even if I screamed, I knew no one would hear me. How could I have been so foolish?

I picked up my basket and was about to catch up with the women, when a man asked, "What's your hurry, little lady?"

When I turned towards the voice, I was shocked to see Cyrus leering at me. My heart froze. Why had he followed me out here? Had he stalked me like an animal? I decided my best option was to act like this was all very normal and carry on with trying to rejoin the women.

"Good day, Mr. Parker. Are you picking berries also?"

There was his sleazy grin again. "Yes, ma'am, and I found a lovely, ripe berry."

"Well, I hope you find more than one. There are piles out here. This is a great spot."

"I've already found the one I was looking for."

With that, Cyrus walked towards me. I started walking away. I had left Sadie at the wagon so she wouldn't get ticks—she seemed to collect them—but now I wished I had brought her. Cyrus grabbed my wrist and knocked my berry basket flying. It was sad to see all my pickings lying on the ground. Cyrus tried to pull me closer. That's when an amazing thing happened.

Lachlan sprang out of nowhere. Yes, Lachlan. He had been stalking the stalker. I don't know if Cyrus knew what hit him. He was knocked out cold in a heartbeat. I couldn't believe it. I am so indebted to that man. We left Cyrus where he fell.

Lachlan spoke with the captain, who then paid the Parkers a visit. From what I understand, they were informed he wouldn't stand for this kind of behavior on his wagon train. He even called Cyrus a snake. When Cyrus came to and got back to his wagon, he would find the rest of the wagons had carried on without him. His folk's wagon would be the only wagon he would see. I feel sorry for the Parkers, but Lachlan said they should have trained their boy better.

Speaking of snakes, Snake River Canyon was incredibly beautiful—but also incredibly deadly. It's a deep gorge that winds for about fifty miles and leads to a dangerous climb over the Blue Mountains. One of the wagons following the steep path plunged over the edge into the Columbia River. It was horrible to watch. The wheels got too close to the edge.

It doesn't sound nearly as bad on paper, but to see a wagon fall off a cliff is terrible. People were screaming and crying, but there was nothing anyone could do. So much of this trip seems like a nightmare. I can't bear to think about it. I just want to go home, but I realize that's impossible.

We hope to reach the settlement of Dalles before winter before going on to Oregon City. I'm not sure how many settlers will arrive at the destination. As I've said, there have been so many deaths. Lachlan is taking his job as my chaperone very seriously these days. He says he is determined to get me safely to my destination. It's wonderful having such a kind man concerned about my well-being. Sometimes he still treats me like a child, but perhaps he is being wiser than I am and only means to protect me. I am so thankful he was keeping an eye on Cyrus.

Abraham is a historian among the pioneers who likes to visit us at dinner time. I don't blame him, he's a lonely, hungry old bachelor. God provides so much food for us, I'm happy to share with anyone needing a meal and company. You'd like him— in fact I wish you could meet him. He's a fine gentleman—and so interesting. He's probably in his late sixties, kind of old for the trail, but he's wiry and spry. He taught history at a college for years, until, like he says, he got "a hankering for adventure."

We must seem like an eager audience because he loves to visit us. He sits around the fire and tells us stories. One story was about a woman he heard who went insane on the trail. He said it was on this very spot, near Snake River. Elizabeth Markham announced to her family one morning that she was not going any farther. She was finished with the Oregon Trail. Her husband had to take the wagons and children and leave her behind because the train was moving on. Mr. Markham must have decided it was wrong to abandon his wife, so when they stopped for lunch, he sent their son back with two horses to get her. I'm not sure why he sent his son and didn't go himself. Maybe he had chores to attend to. Maybe he thought his wife would listen to the lad.

Mr. Markham must have been so surprised to see his wife return on horseback without the boy. Mrs. Markham calmly informed the family she had clubbed the boy to death with a rock. Mr. Markham raced back to retrieve his son. Thankfully, the boy was still alive. When he and his son returned, they found Mrs. Markham had set fire to one of the family's wagons. I'm not sure how the story ends, but perhaps Mrs. Markham was abandoned somewhere else so she couldn't hurt another soul.

Insanity on the trail happens more than you can imagine. Abraham had a strange look on his face as he told that story. I couldn't decipher what his expression was. He almost looked insane himself as he told the story with such wild-eyed enthusiasm. His face suddenly changed. It was as if he was coming back to us from a faraway place. He changed the subject entirely and told the story of Ruth from the Bible in such color it seemed like we were there. I could hear Ruth breathing. I felt her fear at going to a new country, and yet her determination to follow the God of Israel.

It amazes me how God moves behind the scenes, bringing people together in His time for His purposes. Just as God led Ruth into His plans for her life, I believe He orchestrates the events of our lives and leads us in the way He would have us go. It makes me pause and wonder, what does God have planned for my life? I believe His plans for you, my precious Ma, are to bless and encourage every young woman He brings to your door. You sure were a huge blessing and encouragement to me.

The last time Abraham came, he brought about ten flapping quail tied by their legs as a thank you present for all the meals we've provided. We had an extra chicken crate because we ate half our chickens, so the quail reside in that crate now. Have you ever heard a quail's call, Ma? It's such a peculiar sound. It seems the quails pair up and the males guard their females. I don't think I can eat those sweet birds. I just might accidentally leave the cage door open.

We hadn't seen Abraham for about a week. When he visited again, he seemed sad but wouldn't let on why. He sat by the fire for the longest time, just staring into the flame. Something was bothering him. Lachlan asked him about it, but he just shrugged and said "I'm fine."

It was odd, how he suddenly started talking, as if we were in the middle of a conversation. He told us the Oregon Trail really began in 1803 when Lewis and Clark traveled from the Mississippi River to Oregon. Their route was crazy dangerous. Later a man named Robert Stewart, a trapper, traveled ten months from Oregon to Missouri, the route that eventually became the actual Oregon Trail.

Abraham told us that in the 1840's, thousands of trappers, hunters, prospectors, missionaries, and settlers made the trek west along the Oregon Trail. He estimated that for every mile on the two-thousand-mile trek, at least one life was lost. I can't say I'm at all surprised. The trail has improved immensely since Lewis and Clark's expedition, but there's still dangers from wild animals, deadly poisonous snakes, starvation, disease, poison from tainted foods, hazards on the trail, firearm accidents, blizzards and other severe weather conditions like tornados, crazy lightning storms, and hostile Indians. We've seen much of all that.

I didn't know the half of what this trip entailed. If anyone tells you they plan to join a wagon train, please let them read my letters first. They need to count the cost. We have lost over thirty of the fifty wagons we started with. Some left to head back to Independence. They couldn't handle the hardships here. Some of the wagons blew up in a gunpowder explosion, some caught fire and were destroyed, some went over the edge of cliffs, and one floated down a river. I have been traumatized by so much of this. Talking with God, Lachlan, and the women folk are the only things that keep me tethered to this earth and sanity. Tomorrow is my birthday! I can't believe I'll be twenty-two. Life seems to go by so quickly.

I love you, Ma.

Chapter Twelve

July 22, 1854

Dear Ma,

Yesterday, I almost died! *It's a miracle I'm alive to write this to you. Honestly, I thought I was going to be standing in Heaven to meet God. That would be amazing—I would never complain about that—but I'm only twenty-one. Oh wait, it was my birthday—I'm twenty-two—but I still want to teach in Oregon before I go to Heaven. I am not ready to embrace death. I don't want to leave this life before I have a chance to live.*

It's amazing how a life can change in a heartbeat. It was a beautiful summer day. We followed the Bear River to an amazing place called "Soda Springs". It was lovely. There was an abundance of grass for the animals. Natural hot pools of bubbling water were wonderful to bathe in. Lachlan said they were heated by volcanic activity. The clothes seemed to be cleaner than I have ever seen them, maybe because the water is so alkaline. Some of the women joked as they lounged in the hot pools and asked if they had died and gone to Heaven.

Timberly and I were sitting on a rocky ledge by the edge of a deep pool. It was so deep the water was inky black. On one side of the pool, the water flowed over huge boulders, cascaded down a waterfall, then continued along a deep riverbed. It was bath day, so most of the women were in the shallow pools. Only those who could swim sat by the deep water.

The day was scorching hot, so Timberly and I decided to jump in. The water felt like liquid velvet, so soft and warm. Sylvia sat on the edge watching us. She was someone I didn't know well. She rarely spoke. She went everywhere with her sister. I assumed she was a swimmer or she wouldn't be sitting by the deep water. The rest of this story is kind of a blur.

I don't know if Sylvia fell in, the edge was a bit slimy and slippery, or she jumped in, but it was soon obvious the woman in deep water couldn't swim. I don't know how she managed to get to me, I was in the middle of the pool, but she did.

The woman was frantic. She was thrashing violently in the water, and somehow, I don't know how, managed to grab me by the back of my neck. The next thing I knew my neck was being held in a vice grip, and I was being dragged under the water.

The more Sylvia panicked, the tighter her hands clasped my neck. The strength in her hands was unbelievable. I tried, but there was no way I could pry her fingers loose. I was pretty sure if I didn't drown, I would be choked to death. The pain from her hold on my neck was excruciating.

I remember seeing masses of Sylvia's curly blonde hair floating all around me. The hair looked like strands of golden seaweed. Everything started to look golden. The more she thrashed, the deeper we went into the water. The next thing I knew, I was on the bottom of that deep, dark pool. I knew I was drowning and there was nothing I could do.

I had the urge to breathe, but I knew if I did, I would breathe in water. I knew I had to get to the surface and time was running out, but the vice grip on my neck wouldn't let up.

I didn't know if anyone was even aware of what was happening to us. I begged God to please send help.

Instinctively, I tried to push Sylvia up and off my neck. I hoped if she was higher in the water, she would have to let go of my neck and her thrashing would attract someone's attention. I knew if someone didn't rescue us soon, we were both dead. I felt sheer panic but helpless to change anything. I think that's when I started to black out. Everything was so peaceful. I heard what sounded like the rush of angels' wings. Were they there to take me home? My lungs burned. I think we were under the water for less than a minute, but it seemed like we had been there for an eternity. Time had gone into slow motion.

Just as I felt like everything was fading from golden into blackness, and I knew I was on the verge of unconsciousness, a strong hand grabbed me and pulled me to the surface. I took the biggest breath I have ever taken in my life. The air burned my lungs. Every breath brought pain. I wonder if that's what a newborn baby feels, the first time oxygen is in their lungs. No wonder they cry.

I was so disorientated—completely confused. Moments passed. I remember things in pieces—seeing Sylvia lying on the rocks beside me, coughing and vomiting. I must have fainted right after seeing her, as I was unconscious to anything until I woke up on my bed. Lachlan had carried me there.

Even though it was a hot day, I must have been in shock, as I was shivering and cold. He covered me in a warm grizzly hide, but that didn't stop the shivers. Lachlan had such an anxious look on his face, I almost laughed. He gently touched my cheek, and I could hear him murmur, "Dear God, thank You for sparing Rose."

Lachlan told me the rest of the story later. When Sylvia started thrashing in the water, her sister started screaming. Why on earth they were by the deep pool if they couldn't swim is a mystery. The screams alerted the men. Timberly hollered, "It's Rose!" Lachlan was there in seconds. He dove in immediately and grabbed us both. Thank God he is such a strong man. I fully expect to have nightmares of curly blonde hair floating around me.

I thanked Lachlan for rescuing me, and when he heard me speak, he looked concerned and told me to rest my voice. My voice does sound strange—kind of hoarse. I guess that's from the pressure that was on my throat when I was being choked to death. Can you imagine what would have happened if Lachlan hadn't responded to the screams? How can I ever thank him enough?

Ma, I am lying on the bed in our wagon with strict orders to rest. Thankfully, Lachlan approved my writing to you. Writing helps me form my thoughts and see things clearly. It comforts me, because I feel like you are here. It's like we are sitting in the parlor having tea together. I see your kind eyes, your gentle smile. I feel the warmth of your loving spirit. The only thing missing is the real you. It comforts my heart to know I will see you again one day, and we will never be parted for all eternity.

Sadie and Ruby are refusing to let me out of their sight. They are both sitting on my feet as I lie on the bed, staring at me. I have never seen such huge eyes so full of concern. I'm so thankful God created animals.

Lachlan is taking such good care of me. He just brought my supper. I feel so pampered. Honestly, I am so thankful for this man. I am thinking of all the things he has done since I met him. He paid my fare on the wagon train, he paid for all the food and supplies, he looks after the wagon and the animals, he helps look after others on the trail, he chops all our firewood, , he often makes coffee and meals for me, and now he has saved my life.

Honestly, I have never in my life met a man I loved and respected more. Did I just write loved? If I didn't want to waste ink and paper, I'd put this piece in the fire this minute. But I am so grateful to him. Maybe I do love him.

Now I wish you were actually here, so I could ask you what real love looks like. I know you were in love with your Michael. I can understand more how it must have broken your heart when cholera claimed his life before you had a chance to marry. If anything happened to Lachlan—well, it would be devastating.

I must tell you, Ma, Lachlan James Smith is a very kind, thoughtful man. Back in Independence, when he bought supplies for our trip, he also bought a bag of sweets and hid them for a special occasion. Guess what I found lying on my pillow for my birthday? A bag of sweets and a dozen short-stemmed, fragrant prairie roses. So sweet.

Ma, I know you'll be glad to hear this. There are so many precious, godly women on this wagon train. I am so blessed to be surrounded with women who seem determined to help me learn all I can about everything. I had no idea I was so naïve about life. There's a group of us who meet whenever we have a chance. We wash clothes and cook together, pray, sew, and so much more. I love them all dearly. They feel like family.

I love you, Ma.

Chapter Thirteen

Days seemed to blur together. There was a monotony about the journey. Everyone looked tired— bone weary. It was hard to keep one foot plodding in front of the other. Would this journey ever end?

When the women gathered to sew, Rose had an idea. She asked her friends to speak to themselves now, in the present, from their future self. What advice would they give themselves? This creative idea seemed to spark life into dull, bored eyes. The atmosphere changed from heaviness to hilarity, as the women challenged their present selves to look to the future.

Cindy said, "I think my future self would say to my present self don't panic. Trust God. This is only a temporary, light affliction. This too shall pass."

German Oma wisely said, "You can do this. You are almost at the end of this journey. Don't give up! The end of these trials is near. It gets better from here."

Stephanie said, "Never go to bed angry."

Debbey got very excited about the beautiful home her husband was going to build for her. "This covered wagon is not your final home, Debbey. You won't live here for life. Your home will be so big all your friends can come live with you." Everyone laughed.

Connie couldn't help it. She had to say, "Now ladies. This is serious. So your body isn't crippled with unforgiveness and bitterness, don't go to bed angry!"

It was sobering to think that by holding on to unforgiveness, you were destroying yourself.

Renee thought it would be wise to learn to sew better now, so future Renee could make beautiful clothes for herself and others. Oma smiled at her sewing students. All such precious women. They shared a bond of love that had been forged in troubles, in sickness, and sometimes in the presence of death. These women knew that wherever God took them, they would carry each other in their hearts.

It seemed like it was appropriate, so Kathy said, "I love all of you. I hope we see each other again. Wherever I am, my home will always be open to you."

All the women agreed and said they felt the same way. Many said to the group, "You are always welcome in my home."

Jemimah sat quietly. She wasn't sure if all these lovely thoughts included her. Rose noticed her silence, her looking so intently at her sewing, and the pain and confusion on her face. Just because she had been a slave, didn't mean she wasn't a precious daughter of the Most High God. She was a treasure to Him, just as valuable as anyone.

"Jemimah, just so you know, the welcome from all of us includes you also," Rose said.

Jemimah looked up. Her eyes filled with tears as she said, "You all are the best sista's a body could have." At that point, all sewing was dropped so Jemimah could be hugged.

Oma suggested they pray and ask God to help them be strong for the remainder of the journey.

"Dear Heavenly Father," Rory prayed, "Thank You that You love us. Thank You that You promise to be with us always, even to the end of the age."

Cindi said, "Dear Father, I thank You for Your great love."

As the women said "Amen," everything went completely still. Not a bird made a sound. Nothing. Complete quiet. Calm. The sky turned a strange greenish color.

"The calm before the storm," Cindi said.

"Just look at those clouds!" Phyllis hollered. She didn't mean to holler. It made little Ruby scream and Sadie bark. All the women stared at the sky in disbelief. There seemed to be huge, dark fragments of clouds hanging from the sky.

And then—suddenly—a humming sound, like the drone of a million bees, followed by a loud rumble like thunder, and then a deafening roar. They looked towards the noise to see what could have caused it. The sky darkened in moments. One of the cloud fragments dropped violently to the ground in a huge, whirling, dark tunnel of wind. It seemed to be growing in size. It was terrifying but fascinating at the same time.

Betty screamed, "It's a twister! We had them back in Kansas."

"What do we do?"

The sky was getting blacker. The funnel cloud churned with power, seemingly getting bigger by the second.

Oma yelled over the roar, "Find the lowest spot you can and hide!"

Sewing projects were discarded as the women got up and ran. It looked like Rory was running towards her wagon to hide.

"No, Rory, don't go in the wagon!" Rose screamed.

"I've got to get my dog!" Rory hollered back.

"Hurry!" someone yelled.

The tornado was almost upon them. The women plastered themselves in ditches and any low areas they could find.

"Rory, get down!" Rose screamed as the twister smashed into the side of her wagon. It was smashed to pieces in an instant. Sadie howled, women screamed, as the deafening roar passed over them. They could hear twisting and crunching sounds as wood and metal wagons were demolished.

"Dear God, please protect us," Rose prayed.

She could hear women all around her praying.

"Lawd, have mercy. Lawd, have mercy."

Rose recognized Jemimah's voice.

"Lord, I'm so sorry I said things were boring," a voice cried. "Please make it stop!"

Just as suddenly as it came, it disappeared. It seemed like the tornado evaporated. The sun shone brilliantly. It was as if nothing had happened, but when they looked at the wagons, it was obvious something horrific had happened. Four wagons were completely demolished.

Folks walked around the wagons in a daze. How could so much devastation happen in moments? Many walked as if they were in a dream. It was the worst kind of a dream—a nightmare. Folks looked in disbelief at the wagons that lay in splinters.

Captain Whittaker blew his bugle. Folks knew when the bugle blew at any time other than morning it meant they were to gather at the boss's wagon.

Babies cried. Children whined. Adults shouted.

"All right folks, calm down."

The folks didn't calm down. It was complete chaos.

"I SAID CALM DOWN!"

This shouted command hushed all the noise.

"Now, we have a situation here. Four wagons were in the path of the tornado and destroyed. Four families are without a wagon. Any suggestions as to what we should do?"

"Perhaps four singles could sleep under their wagon so a family could use their wagons?" Amos suggested.

There were some murmurs from the single men. Jacob spoke up. He was one of the single men. "I think that's a fair idea."

The captain said, "We have been presented with a wise idea. All in favor say Aye." All voices said "Aye" in agreement.

Hours later, right around the time folks would have been getting ready to prepare the evening meal, the bugle blared again. The trail boss was asking them to assemble again? Twice in one day? That was unheard of.

"Folks," Captain Whittaker said, "This has been quite the day for all of us. We have much to be thankful for. There was no loss of life. I would like the preacher to say a prayer for all of us."

Men folk took their hats off as a sign of respect to God.

The preacher looked pleased to be called upon.

"Dear heavenly Father, we humbly come before you with hearts full of thanksgiving. We are amazed at Your kindness to us. Thank You there was no loss of life this day. Thank You, so many shared what little they had to had to help one another. We are grateful for the love we have seen today. We truly recognize that such love and compassion can only come from Your heart. Please be with us as we continue this journey. In Jesus Name. Amen."

"One more thing—" Captain Whittaker said. "Today is a celebratin' kind of day. There's an ox that doesn't wish to travel another step. She will be cut up and shared with all of you. The single men will bring the meat to your wagons shortly. Please invite them to join you for supper"

There was a cheer that rang through the surrounding woods. The captain had finally earned the respect and admiration he had been craving.

Wednesday, July 26, 1854

Dear Ma,
It took us several days to get to Fort Hall because of an incident we had. A tornado ripped through our wagon train a few days ago. Thankfully, only four wagons were destroyed. No lives were lost. Praise God!

God has used this tornado for good. Folks have shared provisions of food, pots, fry pans, dishes, wooden spoons, blankets, guns, ammunition, and clothing to help one another. It's been amazing.

I feel sorry for Wilma. She couldn't handle the stresses of the trail, so the captain shot her to put her out of her misery. Did I mention Wilma was an elderly, ornery mule?

Lots of folks are having a hard time with their oxen. They have been walking so many hours every day, pulling thousands of pounds, their metal shoes have fallen off, and their hooves are splitting. It must be unbearably painful for them. No wonder so many are quitting. So, once the hooves split, they have to be sealed with hot tar. That must be so painful also.

Sometimes an ox decides he's had enough of this whole wagon train adventure and just stops. Once an ox decides to stop, there's really nothing that will get him going again. Maybe something inside the animal says, "I can't do this. I can't go another step." I understand. There are days I feel that way too.

Some wagons have gone from six oxen down to four. Thankfully we were advised to bring an extra pair, as we're down to four now. Two of them were shared as food with the others as they refused to go another step.

One of the mothers, whose boy I've been helping learn to read, gave me a thank you dress she had been sewing for me. It's funny how she kept it a secret from me for months. I've visited Sarah often in her wagon and never saw a hint of cloth. I've never had a simple cotton dress before. It's a pretty rose color. It felt wonderful putting on a clean dress. My beautiful deep rose dress that I have been wearing night and day can finally be washed.

Lachlan is still insisting I rest. He seems worried about me. He decided to surprise me today. For lunch we had scorched biscuits and cheese. They were delicious. Honestly. Maybe it's because they were made by the kindest man I have ever met. Maybe he is trying to show me he really does need a cook. Just now, as I was writing to you, Lachlan brought me afternoon tea and a hard biscuit—the kind of biscuit you dip in tea and it turns into mush. Usually, it just disintegrates into your tea and your entire cup is filled with mush. It's not that appetizing, but I am so thankful for his care.

There's a precious woman—we call her German Oma— who shares words of wisdom with us younger women. She has been teaching us a lot about marriage and gives great advice about life. The marriage information doesn't relate to me at all. I don't need marital advice, but I listen because there are probably some things I can apply in my single life. It's strange, Ma. I'm probably the oldest single girl on this trail. So many of the brides are years younger than me. Maybe I'll end up a school spinster for after all. I'm already starting to feel old.

Yesterday, as we sat by the fire, Oma gave us a sewing lesson. She has the finest stitches I've ever seen. She seems to be on a "what to do before you go to bed" marital thread. Oma has such wise advice. She said, "Always remember love is a choice."
Really? I'm not choosing to love Lachlan with my head, it's not a conscious choice, it's my heart that loves him. My head is saying, "What are you doing? You can't love him. You will be going separate ways soon." But my heart is saying, "He is so wonderful, so handsome, so kind—" Oh dear. I just realized I wrote all that in your letter. I think what Oma means by her comment is that when the feelings of love aren't there, it becomes a choice to respond in loving ways.

I am still lying on the bed with strict orders to rest, remembering the wise advice the women shared. Oma also said, "Never respond in anger. Count to ten before you reply."

That advice would work well for any relationships. It's not smart to act impetuously. It's wise to decide what is best to say and what is best left unsaid before one speaks. I guess being so fearful of saying the wrong thing and being punished at the orphanage kept me from speaking impetuously, so that was a good thing. There's good to be found in all circumstances, right? I can see you nodding your head in agreement.

Oma also said, "What you do in the early days of marriage sets a precedent, and you may do that for the rest of your marriage."

I wonder how that happens. I guess the things we do can quickly become habits. Like, I am supposed to be the cook, but by the time I am up in the mornings, Lachlan often already has the coffee on and something cooking. His saying he needed a cook along is sounding more and more suspicious. I guess what Oma means is that if we form good habits right away they can become a beautiful part of our relationship. I'm thankful Lachlan gets things ready in the mornings. I think that would be a lovely habit for him to have with whoever he chooses to marry. Interesting, I just felt a pang of grief and sadness thinking about Lachlan marrying someone else. Does that sound strange, Ma?

There were several more women who shared advice. Cindy, said "Always say I love you and kiss at the end of every prayer." *That sounds lovely.* She also said, "Communicate with each other and work things out. *That feels like it would heal most misunderstandings.* Cindy also said, "Always take time for yourself, time together, and time with God. Never expect your man to read your mind. Communication is the key. Bring it all to God. The good and bad and ugly. You can share with wise women in your life or your pastor, but never talk bad about your husband or let others think bad about him. He needs and wants your respect almost more than love! No one's perfect. Not him. Not you. Always say I love you, and kiss at the end of every prayer." *Such wonderful advice.*

Stephanie, advised, "Never go to bed angry at your spouse." *I can't imagine being angry at Lachlan. I suppose that could happen, but at this moment it is unimaginable.*

Renee said, "Always say I love you. Never go to bed angry (there it is again!!!)...and something else...marriage is a two-person adventure. Give and accept."

Connie said, "Love is patient. Don't go to bed angry." *Ma, there must be a reason the Bible says, "Don't let the sun go* down on your wrath." Does it fester overnight and create a bigger mess?

Debbey has wise advice. "Always seek God first in everything. Never forget to pray together, and for each other. Remember to make many memories."

I am sure Lachlan and I have made more memories in these few months than most married folks make in a lifetime. The memory of his rescuing me from Cyrus saving my life will be with me for the rest of my life. Did I mention blonde, wavy hair scares me a bit now?

Kathy had great advice. She said, "People should always say please, thank you, I appreciate you, and I love you. Never go to bed angry with one another. Pray, and turn it over to God." This part sounds almost like it's from King Solomon's lips. "Have fun, and spend your short lives together, placing God first, and always remember how much you love one another."

Betty said, "Never go to bed angry, and you can never say 'I love you' too many times."

Kim advised, "Always love yourself first, never go to bed angry. "Give it all to God, and have fun doing life." It seems there must be a lot of anger in marriage, because a lot of the advice is about being angry. I have never seen Lachlan angry. Even when the men came to rob us in the middle of the night, Lachlan seemed more amused with them than mad. He seemed to think it was funny they thought they would get away with their plans.

Rory said, "Never go to sleep mad at your partner. Love with all your heart. Talk to each other and compromise. Love God and make Him first in your life."

Phyllis said, "Always build your husband up. Never air your disagreements with each other—which you will have—in public. Keep them private out of respect for each other."

Marcia said, "Never let your husband leave without a kiss and I love you. Who knows what the day should hold—" That's so true. That's obvious here on the trail. Lives can be changed in a heartbeat.

Crystal said, "Always remember to communicate. Never go to bed angry. You can't change the other person no matter how hard you try."

Wendy said, "Always show your love through the little things you do." Here it is again… "Never go to bed angry with each other…and always say I love you."

Ma, all the great advice reminds me of talking with you. I miss you. I would love to be sitting with you and hearing your advice about life right about now.

Owen and Willow invited us over for my birthday dinner. I couldn't have it on my actual birthday because I was recovering from nearly drowning, so they decided to celebrate today. I think a chef in a fancy restaurant would have a hard time competing with Willow's creations. Lachlan said she told him she is making fry bread and wild rice with prairie chicken stew. She is an amazing cook. Lachlan carried me down from the wagon, and probably would have carried me all the way to his brother's wagon if I hadn't insisted I was fine and able to walk.

At night you can feel a chill in the air. It feels like winter is coming. Some of the trees have started to turn color in the highest parts of the trail. That gives me a feeling of dread. We left in April so we could be in Oregon before the snow. I don't think many are prepared for snow. I know I'm not. Ma, if you get this letter one day, you know I was alive and able to send it to you. If we had known about the dangers that would face us, we would have wondered if coming on this journey in the first place was a sensible thing to do at all.

Honestly, Ma, I am so blessed to be friends with these precious, godly women. I can hardly believe it's my birthday celebration today. My friends made a massive molasses stack cake for me. Ma, all the great advice reminds me of talking with you. I miss you. I would love to be sitting with you and hearing your advice about life right about now.

I love you, Ma

Chapter Fourteen

"Lachlan, when you were a little boy, what did you want to be when you grew up?" Rose asked.

"I thought I'd have a business of some kind. Maybe a cattle ranch."

"And that dream never left you"

"I looked at my options. I didn't want to be a miner, a banker, a lawman, or a prospector. Being a rancher sounded like a good fit for me."

"I think you will be a fine rancher. You take such good care of our animals."

Rose realized with surprise she called them "our animals." They clearly all belonged to Lachlan. But he didn't seem to mind or even notice she had said that.

"Lachlan, it's funny, but I feel like I am still waiting for my life to begin. I feel like all the things I have done have been preparation for my real life that is yet to come."

"I trust God's plans for you are good, Rose."

Tuesday, August 15, 1854

Dear Ma,
We arrived in Fort Boise late at night. The captain intends to give us a rest day tomorrow. We need it.

I'm thankful for Willow's cooking lessons. It's actually quite incredible that my food tastes good. Maybe it's because we are so grateful for everything God gives us that burnt biscuits aren't so bad. Nothing is taken for granted. We realize so clearly out here, how our lives are in God's hands.

I haven't told you about the trees. They are beautiful. I'm so thankful God made trees. Cottonwoods grow along the lakes, rivers, and streams in the low areas. When we get into higher elevations we are among fir and pines. I love the clean, fragrant smell of the evergreens.

There's a strange tree called the Osage orange that grows along the trail. The fruit is like a green orange and it's extremely bitter. I've been using it with sugar to make a kind of lemonade. I thought that would help keep scurvy away. I told Lachlan it's his medicine, and he's dutifully drinking it. He makes the most hilarious faces.

Ma, this is being written several days after my last entry. If I'd thought I had horrible things happen before, it was nothing compared to this.

I was out collecting Osage fruit by the river, when a hand was clasped over my mouth and I was swung up onto a horse. I couldn't see the person who was abducting me. The hand was kept over my mouth, so I wasn't able to scream for help.

Eventually, I was deposited in a teepee that reeked of wood smoke and a strong smell I didn't recognize. Maybe it was some kind of sweet grass tobacco. The teepee was filled with dried gourds full of dried berries and buffalo jerky. Huge buffalo hides were attached to the sides of the teepee and covered the floor.

A woman who looked about fifty spoke with me. She spoke slowly, as if she thought I wouldn't understand English.

"We are from the Nez Perce Nation. We are called Nimiipu, "The People." We breeders of fine horses. We created Appaloosa."

When I asked why I was there, she said, "You will marry brave warrior bring you here."

"Why?"

"He son. He want you wife. He watched you days."

"But I don't want to marry him."

"If person comes buy you today, you free. If not, marry son tonight."

The woman left, then returned with a bowl of berries and dried beef. There was no way I could eat anything. I begged God to send Lachlan.

"Rest. You help with fish soon."

I thought if she wants me to catch fish she will see how useless I am and send me back to the wagon train.

The teepee was filled with dried gourds full of dried berries and buffalo jerky. Huge buffalo hides were attached to the sides of the teepee and covered the floor.

About an hour later, a warrior came into the tent. He smiled at me and reached out his hand for me to take it. I was honestly petrified, but I felt I had no choice. He led me out of the teepee to the river.

I watched the men use spears and nets to catch fish. I was given a knife and told, "You clean fish." I had no idea what to do. I watched the other women and tried to copy them.

As we cleaned, I heard horse's hooves coming up behind me. I turned to look. Guess who it was? If you guessed Lachlan, you were right. My hero. My heart leaped with joy. He was leading a goat with a rope.

"Greetings. I come in peace."

Several warriors stood at attention, prepared to hurl their spears into him if needed.

"I have come to buy the woman. She is my woman, but I will pay you for her."

Ma, I couldn't believe he said, "my woman." I have never heard sweeter words. The warriors talked among themselves. It seemed like there was an argument. The man who brought me from the tent, I assume my intended groom, was obviously not pleased with this new development. He was loudly expressing his displeasure. One finally spoke.

"Why we give you woman? We take goat, kill you, keep woman."

"You could, but then you would miss getting the other valuable treasures I have to give you. This goat is to show I am willing to trade. I have more to give at my camp."

"Go get this more…"

"No, you must give me the woman and come to my camp. I will give you gifts there."

The men got back into a circle. The air buzzed with the sound of their voices.

The groom had already stalked off. He stood at a distance, glaring at Lachlan. I prayed God would keep Lachlan safe.

"We accept. We follow to camp. If gifts acceptable, we trade gifts for woman."

I was filled with thankfulness, then I wondered what he was planning to give up for me. I got to ride on the stallion with "my man." Four Nez Perce Indians rode with us. I was surprised how close we were to the wagon train.

The Indians were offered almost all the animals we had left: the cow, a goat Lachlan had purchased for a bag of grain, a pig, and five chickens, everything except Sadie and Ruby. Each warrior had something to bring back to the camp. They accepted the trade. As soon as the warriors were out of sight, I burst out crying.

"Lachlan, how can I ever thank you enough?"

"Rose, I couldn't lose you. I would have given up everything I own to keep you safe."

I was still sobbing while Lachlan held me in his arms and cried also.

"How did you find me?"

"I prayed before following the freshest tracks I could find. I thank God I found you."

"I thank God you found me too."

Ma, I owe Lachlan my life—twice now. I don't know how I can ever thank him enough.

Our preacher had such a good message for us from James 1:2-4 last Sunday. It was so encouraging.

"Consider it pure joy, my brothers and sisters, whenever you face trials of many kinds, because you know that the testing of your faith produces perseverance. Let perseverance finish its work so that you may be mature and complete, not lacking anything."

It's true, Ma. When trials arise, God is giving us the opportunity to develop patience. I've had more trials in the past few months than most people have in a lifetime. I need wisdom from Him to survive this journey. People are so afraid now. There have been so many deaths. Disease is common on the trail. The hardships of the journey, the diet without fresh produce, and the ever-present exhaustion make folks vulnerable to horrible diseases such as cholera, flu, dysentery, measles, mumps, scarlet fever, tuberculosis, and typhoid fever. All can bring death to an entire wagon train. Thankfully, we've only had dysentery. Did I mention cholera comes from dirty water? It's actually a miracle we haven't had that and aren't all dead as most of the water we've seen doesn't look clean. I boil the water before we use it, but that doesn't always help.

Food poisoning is an ever-present issue. I went to get bacon out of a barrel of sawdust a while back and it was crawling with maggots. It was a sickening thought knowing we had eaten some of it the day before. It's hard to keep food from being contaminated.

Another issue we were informed about at the last fort is scurvy. We were told the disease makes a person feel tired and weak, irritable, and sad. It causes severe leg cramps, makes the gums swell up and bleed, and can even cause people's teeth to fall out. So far, thank God, we haven't had any issues with that disease.

I am trusting God, that He will lead us safely to our new home.

I love you, Ma.

Chapter Fifteen

Lachlan was surprised to see Jemimah coming for coffee so early in the morning. As soon as she was perched on a stump by the fire, holding a coffee mug, she burst out, "Lachlan, I hasta to talk to you. It's 'bout a dream I had—a bad dream"

"A bad dream?"

"A scary dream. It's 'bout Missy."

"Oh?"

"Lawd, have mercy. It's a warnin' from God."

"Rose?" Lachlan felt his stomach convulsing.

"I heared 'bout a attack on Rose's life. I pray God protects tha' woman. Dear God, thank You that You has not given me a spirit of fear, but of power, love, and a sound mind."

"What did God show you?"

"I seen Rose standin' in a deep valley. Looked like millions of soldiers comin' 'gainst her—dressed in red—hurlin' daggers—tryin' to steal her breath. Them soldiers was so evil, just wantin' only to rob, steal, kill and destroy."

"What else did you see?"

"I seen Rose fall—she stopped breathin'."

"Was she dead?"

"Most nearly."

"Then what?"

"Somethin' strange happened."

"What?"

"I seen you. You was spoonin' water into her mouth. Her breath stopped. You cried out "NO!" That scream brought Rose back—back to breathin'. The Lawd, He used your voice to call that there woman back from death."

"Thank you, Jemimah, for warning me. You're a faithful friend."

"I hasta. It's urgent, for ma Missy. Somethin' terrible Is gonna happen to ma Missy. To save her, you hasta be there."

Wednesday, August 16, 1854

Dear Ma,

I can't believe Fort Boise was only built a few years ago. It already looks worn out and tired—like it's seen too much. I saw a paper tacked up on a bulletin board outside the general store. Didn't the person who put it there realize this was the Oregon Trail? Was he trying to scare folks? I don't think I'll show Lachlan. He's already tired and discouraged. The message said it was written by an anonymous Settler. It was full of horror stories.

Ma, the hardships have been almost unbearable. I've seen many grown men and women cry. Lachlan and I have comforted many a folk who said they just couldn't go on. Maybe it wasn't the most encouraging advice, but it seemed like wise counsel to tell them to just take the next step. Don't quit.

Abraham often talked with us when he felt lonely. He knew he was always welcome at our fire, so what happened is unthinkable. He was like a grandpa to me. He was kind and wise, so what happened makes no sense at all. We thought he had reserves of courage and strength to draw from. We thought he would endure to the end of the trail. He had already survived so much. Maybe it was the sheer boredom of his days, the weight of the work, or maybe he decided he was too tired to go on. I'm sorry we didn't see the signs of depression. They must have been there.

I'm so sad to tell you this, Ma. Abraham took his own life. I hope it was an accident, but the men who found him said it looked deliberate. His wagon was on fire. Maybe they could have lied to us and told us it looked like an accident. That would have been easier.

To say Lachlan and I are in shock is an understatement. Abraham was our friend. I can't begin to understand what would possess a man to kill himself. It kind of reminds me of the story he told us about Mrs. Markham. Was our friend insane? He will be greatly missed.

Did I mention to you the dust is unbearable? It is everywhere, sometimes about three inches thick (I am not exaggerating). Sometimes I have to wear a scarf over my face or it would be impossible to breathe.

Lots of folks are having a hard time with their oxen. They have been walking so many hours every day, pulling thousands of pounds, their metal shoes have fallen off, and their hooves are splitting. It must be unbearably painful for them. No wonder so many are quitting. We have had lots of ox meat dinners as a wagon train, but we would have preferred to have them alive. So, once the hooves split, they have to be sealed with hot tar. That must be so painful also.

I love you, Ma.

Cholera was in the camp. It struck like lightning. Rose had seen this disease before. It struck in a heartbeat and spread rapidly through the orphanage when she was a little girl. It killed many. The victims had watery diarrhea that caused dehydration and often death. Someone said there was an antidote, laudanum. It later became known as opium. This disease was spread from contaminated water and food. A buffalo carcass had been seen floating in the spring. What options did the settlers have? They needed water, so were forced to drink from the spring. The reaction was swift. Most of the camp was sick. They would lose valuable time if they didn't continue, but they couldn't move. There were too many sick.

Folks who were able sat around the fire, wondering how this adventure was going to end. Owen turned to speak to his brother. "Lachlan, I don't know about Marcus. He's supposed to be the assistant trail boss, but he said the train is going to head in a southerly direction in the morning."

Rose said, "That doesn't sound wise."

They had to be through the Rockies before the end of summer. Going south would keep them from crossing the Rockies longer. The trail boss knew the land like the back of his hand. He would never have taken them south. He would have wanted to cross the mountains before there was a risk of snow. But there was one problem. Captain Whittaker was dead —a victim of cholera—and no one knew the route but him. The maps were all in his head. His hired hand assumed the lead. He had no idea where the trail was.

"God, we need You desperately."

Wednesday, August 30, 1854

Dear Ma,

My last entry was two weeks ago. We haven't left Fort Boise. This journey west is definitely not for the faint of heart. It's had difficulties right from the start. Folks encounter their first hardship when they have to leave friends and family behind. They knew they would likely never see them again in this lifetime. But that's just the beginning of grief.

Folks in the last fort informed us some wagon trains have to pass without stopping, because diseases are so rampant. We told them we had already experienced that, when the gates of Fort Bridger were locked to us because several of our folks had dysentery. They also said some wagon trains have lost two-thirds of their people to cholera. It just sweeps through and kills folks in a day. Lachlan said that certainly would give people incentive to get right with God, knowing they could be standing before Him in a few short hours.

We had no idea that within a few days after hearing about cholera, that horrible disease would hit us. People are too sick to move. It's such a scary disease. It could attack a healthy person around breakfast time, and by lunch or dinner time, he would be in a grave. There is no cure we know of for the disease.

The symptoms are terrible—severe diarrhea, vomiting, and leg cramps. Folks would become dehydrated, then septic shock, and even death came within hours. Most folks die in terrible pain within twenty-four hours, but some folks linger in agony, pain, and misery for weeks in the wagons before the die.

Captain Whittaker died of cholera. What is especially tragic about his death is, he was the only one who knew the route. He had the map in his head. The men said we will continue to follow the wagon tracks others have left to the south. Hopefully they weren't lost too. Following their tracks only works as long as there's no snow.

Henry and Gabriella Johnston headed out as part of our wagon train with their seven children. They planned to homestead in Oregon. Sadly, when cholera hit, their family was wiped out in a day. Their infant son was the only survivor. Owen and Willow now have a beautiful baby son. They named him Seth, in honor of their baby son in Heaven. Thankfully, because Willow had so recently lost her baby, she was able to nurse the child. I have never seen two more joyful parents. Owen collected things from the Johnston's wagon, personal items to keep for baby Seth. One day he will want to know about his birth family.

I love you, Ma.

Chapter Sixteen

Someone ran screaming towards Rose. She heard the wailing long before anyone was in sight.

Rose looked up from stirring the pot of beans. She was startled to see her friend looking so distraught.

"What's wrong, Jemimah?"

"Missy—I—need—your—help!"

Her words came out in broken gasps.

"It's the—papers! My freedom papers! They's gone!"

"How could they be gone?"

"They's just gone. I ain't sure where—. Them Pringles say I's still a slave. They say I belong to them."

"But the Pringles know you had them."

"Pringles say I never had 'em."

"The captain saw them—oh, but he's dead."

"Without them papers, I ain't got no proof I's a free woman, Missy."

"That's terrible, Jemimah. I can't believe they'd say that."

"Me neither, Missy. The Lawd knows I's a free woman."

"Pringles know the truth, Jemimah. Let me go with you to talk to them. I'm sure we can sort this out. They're good, honest folk."

Lachlan was under the wagon—greasing the axles—so he was nearby when Rose called.

"Lachlan! We need you!"

Lachlan came out from under the wagon, wiping his hands on his pants.

"What's the matter?"

"It's Jemimah. She can't find her freedom papers, and the Pringles are claiming she's still a slave."

"That's ridiculous. They know she's free."

"She has no proof, Lachlan. Will you come with us to talk to them?"

"I'd be glad to."

When they arrived at the Pringles, it was obvious neither Mr. or Mrs. Pringle wanted to talk. Their faces said, "Get outta here. Mind your own business!"

Their eyes were hostile and their lips were pursed into a tight grimace. Mr. Pringle crossed his arms and stood glaring at the party.

"Whatcha doin' here?"

"Jemimah says there's a misunderstanding."

"What'd she tell you?"

"She says her freedom papers have been mislaid and you're claiming she's not free at all."

"There ain't no misunderstandin'. That's true. She ain't free. She ain't got no freedom papers."

"You know that ain't true!" Jemimah screamed.

Mr. Pringle just stood laughing. He sneered at Jemimah knowing she had no proof.

Just then, Rose noticed little Horace Pringle, hands on his hips, holding a handful of crumpled papers.

Rose slowly edged over towards Horace. Meanwhile, Mr. and Mrs. Pringle were too busy arguing with Lachlan to notice.

"Hi, Horace. What have you got there?" Rose asked sweetly.

Horace made a nasty face and stuck out his tongue.

That didn't stop Rose. She snatched the papers out of his hands in the hopes they were the missing freedom papers.

Little Horace wailed. His screams attracted his parents' attention.

"What are you doing to my sweet boy?" Mrs. Pringle demanded.

Suddenly the Pringles' faces went white with shock. What was Rose holding?

"Give me those papers!" Mr. Pringle shouted as he lunged at her.

Lachlan was not going to stand for anyone hurting Rose. He reached out and grabbed Mr. Pringle by his greasy collar.

"Go back to the wagon, Rose. Take Jemimah with you. I'll deal with these folks."

Lachlan came back shortly after dealing with Pringles. He had spoken with German Oma and arranged for Jemimah to travel with her for the remainder of the journey. It wasn't safe for Jemimah to stay with the Pringles.

"Lachlan, guess what I found?'

"Freedom papers?"

"Yes indeed. Jemimah's a free woman. These papers say so."

"Jemimah, do you want us to keep these papers for you?"

"I's fine to keep 'em now." Jemimah beamed through her tears. "Thank you fo' all you've done. Lawd, I love you both."

Friday, September 1, 1854

Dear Ma,

We had the craziest, scariest thing happen the other day. A mangy, hungry coyote decided to stalk a child. A baby was in a basket on a rock near the edge of a river. His Ma was scrubbing laundry on the rocks. No one noticed the animal. No one actually saw what took place, it happened so fast, we had to piece it all together after. The coyote must have had the basket in his mouth and tried to escape with the child. The baby screamed. Sadie ran at the coyote with such fury, the critter dropped the basket, yelping as it ran into the forest. The baby was saved. As you can probably imagine, Sadie is now the hero of the wagon train. I don't think she has ever been patted or fed so much.

As we left the river, I noticed Ruby had a bloody wound on her back. We couldn't figure out how she got that. She is such a sweet, affectionate baby raccoon – I love her so much— it is hard to see her in pain. She is looking at me so sadly as I write this. I feel so helpless. Her eyes are pleading for me to do something. It is so heart-wrenchingly sad to see her eyes saying, "Please, won't you help me?" It looks like she must have played a part in the coyote story too. It's really so strange no one saw any of the event. Was the coyote after Ruby, and then decided to go for the child instead? I guess we'll never know. Sadie seems beside herself trying to comfort her little friend. I am so thankful God brought this gentle dog into my life. I don't know what will happen when we get to Oregon. Lachlan and I both love her. I can't imagine what life would be like without her. I don't know how we will ever decide who gets to keep her...

That evening, just before she climbed into the wagon, Rose asked "Lachlan, what's wrong with Ruby? She's acting very strange—and there's foam coming out of her mouth."
"I'll check on her."
Moments later Lachlan appeared at the wagon door.
"Hand me my gun."
"Why? What are you going to do?"
"Ruby has rabies. I have to shoot her."
Rose burst out crying.
"No!"

Saturday, September 2, 1854

Ma, I am continuing the letter from a day ago. We have a sorrowful situation here. It's obvious our little chubby Ruby, our sweet baby raccoon, has rabies. She must have got that when that mangy coyote sunk his teeth into her back. I don't know if she can recover...Ma, I'm crying as I write this many hours and many tears later. When Lachlan tried to separate Ruby from Sadie, he found that nearly impossible. Sadie stood in front of Ruby, shielding her from the man with the gun. Lachlan asked me to call Sadie over. This was the first time she disobeyed. She wouldn't leave Ruby. It was horrible, Ma. While Sadie tried to shield Ruby from Lachlan, she suddenly let out a blood curdling howl. Ruby had fastened her teeth into the back of Sadie's leg. The pain of knowing her friend bit her was probably greater than the pain she felt in her leg. Sadie must have realized then something was very wrong with her Ruby. When Sadie turned to look at Ruby, the look on her face was, "My Ruby. My sweet friend. Why did you bite me?" Sadie limped out of the way, partially dragging her wounded leg. Lachlan had a clear shot at our Ruby. I was heartbroken. Sadie's baby friend lay dead. Sadie limped back over, lay beside Ruby, and howled mournfully. It was the saddest thing to see. She refused to eat or drink anything for days. She grieved the loss of her adopted daughter and friend.

I wrote all the above two weeks ago. This has me worried, Ma—and afraid. Sadie's had a fever for days. She doesn't seem to be hungry at all, and she has been drooling excessively. Everything seems to make her jump. I have never seen her act so nervous. Lachlan said she must be tied to the back of the wagon and I am not to go near her. He suspects she has rabies.

I hoped Sadie would be fine, but when I took some dinner to her she lunged at me, growling and snapping. It was hard to believe this was my gentle girl. Lachlan heard the commotion and came to see what was happening. He said he was going to get his gun. No!!! Ma, I can't bear the thought of losing Sadie. I have been praying this over and over. "Dear God, please could Sadie live?" God chose not to answer my prayer. We buried Sadie in a quiet spot by the river. My heart feels like it's breaking. Why did God allow her to die?

I'm sad Adam and Eve chose to disobey God. They had no idea the heap of misery they were bringing on all people—on all creation—for all time. Thankfully, one day the lion will lie down with the lamb. There will be peace and no more killing—ever. I can't wait for that day. I miss you and love you, Ma.

Chapter Seventeen

Rose tossed deliriously on her bed. Her throat was parched—burning. As the prairie schooner bumped over the sagebrush and prairie dog mounds, Willow sat beside her, desperately trying to keep her cool.

"It's okay, Rose. You'll be fine."

Willow said the words with her mouth, but her face said, "I don't know if she's going to live."

After the wagons were in their nightly circle, Lachlan thanked Willow and took his place sitting by Rose. Jemimah asked if she could help, but Lachlan wanted to stay by Rose. He anxiously tried to get Rose to drink some water.

He held it to her parched lips. "Rose, try to drink."

Rose just lay on the bed and moaned. Her forehead felt like it was on fire. There was a deep, scarlet rash across her face. It looked like a bad sunburn. Lachlan touched her cheek. It felt like burning, hot sand. In spite of the fact that she was burning up, Rose was shivering. He covered her with the grizzly hide, the warmest blanket he could find.

"Dear God, please don't let this precious woman die."

He didn't mean to, but he whispered, "I love her, God."

Lachlan spooned water between Rose's parched lips. Suddenly, her breathing stopped.

"NO!" Lachlan screamed. "Rose, come back!"

It was exactly like Jemimah's dream. God had warned them.

She seemed to gasp for a breath and then began breathing.

"A few hours later, a voice from outside the wagon called, "How's Rose?"

Lachlan opened the flap and saw Owen and Willow standing there. Baby Seth was strapped on Willow's chest.

"How is she?"

She's burning up, but she's shivering like she's freezing."

"Let me see her."

Lachlan reached out to help his sister-in-law into the wagon. Willow's hands gently covered Rose's cheeks. She prayed quietly, "Dear God, precious Lord of all creation, hear my prayer."

Lachlan was speechless. He didn't know Willow prayed— or even believed in God.

Willow continued. "Living God, Mighty Chief Cornerstone, please touch Your precious daughter and heal her body."

"What's the matter with her?"

"Lachlan, this is scarlet fever. I've seen it before. It has taken down many strong men. Someone must sit with her all night and put cool cloths on her. If her fever doesn't come down, she will die."

"I will sit with her."

"Lachlan, you cannot. If you are awake all night, who will collect the oxen and put the wheels on the wagon? I brought you food. Owen has it for you. You must eat and stay strong and sleep. May I stay with her tonight?"

"Of course. Thank you."

Owen stood by the fire waiting for Lachlan. He held a bowl of stew and some Johnny cake. "You've got to keep up your strength."

"I can't lose her, Owen. I love her."

"I know. Please come sleep in my wagon tonight. There's an extra bed. Willow will be with Rose. You won't sleep if you hear Rose tonight."

"You're right. Thanks." He was so worried he barely noticed the mosquitos trying to eat him alive.

Lachlan tossed fretfully on the bed. He couldn't sleep. How was he going to protect her and keep this woman alive? That's when he whispered, "I can't protect her, Lord. She's in Your hands."

Lachlan lay listening to a child crying in the night. Coyotes, or perhaps wolves, howled on the surrounding hills. Owls hooted in the distance. He prayed the scarlet fever would die—not Rose.

Early the next morning, before the stars faded into the dawn, Lachlan paced outside the wagon, anxiously waiting to hear how Rose was. Willow sat by her side, putting cold cloths on her face.

"It's okay, Lachlan. The fever is almost gone. The bright scarlet is leaving her face. She's going to live."

Lachlan was so relieved he burst out crying. "God, thank You."

Willow sat with Rose all day. When the fever finally broke, Willow lay on the spare bed and slept. Both women slept all night.

The next morning, Lachlan was startled to see Rose trying to climb down from the wagon. He rushed over to help her.

"Rose, you look so much better. How are you feeling?"

She smiled. It wasn't one of her radiant smiles, it was a weaker, tired smile, but he was thrilled with it. He was relieved to see the brilliant red had gone out of her cheeks.

"I'm fine, thanks. Just a bit dizzy. Why is Willow sleeping in our wagon, Lachlan?"

He liked the sound of that. Our wagon. "She's been looking after you for days."

"Really? Why?"

"You nearly died."

Rose looked like she was going to faint, so Lachlan held out his arm to steady her. He slowly walked her to a stump by the fire and helped her sit. Relief was clearly written all over his face. "You look so much better, Rose," he said again. "May I get you coffee?"

"That would be nice. Thank you."

Holding the tin cup of hot coffee, sitting by the morning fire, Rose watched Lachlan hitch the oxen. He piled his bedding in the back of the wagon. She thought about the things Willow told her.

"That man spent hours going to the creek to collect cold water for you. He was so afraid you were going to die."

Rose was grateful for his kindness, but she felt more than gratefulness. She had tried to get up then, she wanted to thank Lachlan, but Willow had gently made her lie down again. "It's okay, Rose. You can thank him in the morning."

Now it was morning. It seemed like Rose was looking at him with new eyes. The kindness and love she had seen in his eyes made something in her chest ache. What was that? It was a deep longing…but for what? This was a feeling she didn't recognize.

"We'll be moving out soon. Are you going to be okay until noon? Is there anything I can get for you?"

When he looked at her, there was a strange look in his eyes she didn't recognize.

"Rose, you scared me the last two nights. I thought you were going to die."

There was a moment of complete silence, then Lachlan whispered, "I couldn't stand to lose you, Rose."

Rose stared at her coffee mug. It was suddenly very intriguing. She didn't dare look up. What could she say to this? Did she need to say anything? Why did she suddenly feel so confused…so unable to think? Thankfully, the signal was given that it was time to move out. The first wagons were already rolling.

"Rose, let me help you into the wagon. Willow promised to stay with you until you are completely better. She prayed for you…"

Rose smiled slightly. As she stood she started to swoon again. Lachlan swung her up into his arms and carried her to the wagon. As she leaned her head upon his chest, she could feel his heart beating. He lay her gently on the bed and kissed her forehead. That was the last thing she remembered until she woke that evening to the sound of coyotes singing to the moon.

Rose pushed the tarp out of the way and was shocked to see it was pitch dark except for the fire Lachlan sat in front of.

Owen sat with him. As soon as he saw her, Lachlan leaped to his feet and strode towards her.

"Let me help you, little lady." Strong arms gently lifted her to the ground. Rose marveled at how safe and protected she felt in those arms. He carried her to the fire and gently placed her on a stump. Willow appeared in the wagon doorway. Owen went over to help her down.

"We'd best be going," Owen said.

"Thank you so much for all you've done," Lachlan said as two of the dearest people on Earth held hands and walked slowly towards their wagon.

"I made some deer stew," Lachlan told Rose. "Would you like some? It's not as good as yours, but it will give you strength."

"I'm supposed to be cooking for you."

Lachlan's entire face smiled. His eyes seemed to be holding some mysterious secret.

"Rose, you've been so sick. I'm just thankful you're getting better."

Rose smiled at the cook as she was handed a bowl of gruesome looking stew. Cooking was definitely not one of his skills. They sat quietly, listening to the sounds of the night. Crickets kept the main beat, while night birds occasionally added their voices. It was so peaceful. Rose thought,

I feel enveloped in the love of God.

"Rose?"

"Yes, Lachlan...?

"I can't tell you how relieved I am that you're alive."

Rose blushed.

Dear God, I've never had such feelings before. Do I love this man? Is this what love feels like? I've only known him a few months. Is that long enough to love someone?

These new, strange feelings beat savagely in her chest, demanding to be recognized. Rose was determined to suppress these feelings. They felt too dangerous. They frightened her. She had denied her feelings since she was a child in the orphanage. She had learned that expressing feelings was dangerous. It led to punishment. She was afraid of her emotions.

Rose allowed her thoughts to wander. When did the pain begin that made her decide emotions were too scary? Why did they have to be kept locked away? It was definitely at the orphanage. Rose thought of all the lonely days, feeling unloved and unwanted. Was she really only four years old when the darkness invaded her soul? She had made her voice be quiet. Even though she was treated better than most of the other orphans, there was less chance of being beaten or starved if she said nothing. Perhaps, if she was very quiet and very obedient, she would get an extra slice of bread. She couldn't understand why the mistress seemed to despise her—to despise all the children.

Rose remembered the day the Murphys came looking for a child. She had long given up the notion that she would ever be adopted. It was impossible. No one adopted a fourteen-year-old. She was shocked when she was called into Miss Shultz's office for an interview. She was even more shocked when an hour later she was pulled away from peeling potatoes and told to pack her two dresses. The Murphys wanted her! She wasn't sure if she should be scared or rejoice. The Murphys wanted her? Why? Was it possible she would be loved? Maybe they just wanted a servant.

The Murphys treated her kindly. They told her she was their daughter and she was a replacement for their daughter who had recently died of scarlet fever. They felt giving another girl a home and a family is what their Emily would have wanted. In honor of Emily, Rose was given her room, her clothes, her possessions. They told her she looked like Emily, with long dark hair and hazel-colored eyes. Sometimes they accidentally called her Emily. It was a strange feeling, being a replacement for a dead person. She couldn't tell them that. They wouldn't understand. She continued to ignore her feelings and closely guard her thoughts.

Suddenly plunged into a life of opulence, she felt a bit like Joseph, going from a prison to a palace. She now had a beautiful home, silk gowns and slippers, delectable foods cooked by servants, and her dream, the chance to become a teacher. Thankfully that had been Emily's dream too, so it was welcomed.

She was grateful for their kindness, but something was missing. Something she vaguely remembered seeing in her parent's eyes. Love. Was it possible that's what she saw in Lachlan's eyes? The pain of her past made her vulnerable to the appearance of love. She would have to guard her heart.

Rose realized she had developed the habit of looking at life as if she was merely a spectator. She felt her whole life—well, except for the last two years at the rooming house with Ma Morgan—had been spent walking on eggshells. She had to walk cautiously so nothing broke. Would God give her the courage to crush the eggshells and really live?

Jemimah joined them for dinner that night. She was so thankful these white folk didn't seem to notice her skin was darker than theirs. Some white folks had a problem with the color of someone's skin.

Jemimah helped cook dinner. The roasted chicken with onion fried potatoes was delicious. Rose had collected some sage and brewed the leaves in a pot to make sage tea. It made such flavorful tea.

"Thank you, Rose. You're a mighty fine cook," Lachlan said as he placed his plate on the ground. He gave Rose a look that said, "I told you you'd learn." Why did Rose feel she was melting inside whenever he smiled at her? Did Lachlan hold her gaze longer than necessary, or was she imagining it? That man's gaze—

Rose held out her tin cup as Lachlan poured the sage tea for her. He smiled at her and didn't notice he was still pouring the hot tea until Rose screamed and dropped the cup. Lachlan looked so alarmed Rose couldn't help but laugh. She laughed so hard she started to cry. Then, suddenly, surprisingly, a dam burst inside her. All the pain that had been stored in her heart, all the unshed tears from so many years, all gushed out. Lachlan's bewildered face made her laugh and cry even more.

"Rose, are you okay?"

Jemimah looked startled by all that was happening. "Well, I best be going now."

"Night, Jemimah," Lachlan said.

"Night, friends. You's the dearest friends a body could have."

Once she left, Lachlan asked, "Rose, what was that all about? Why were you crying?"

Now that the storm was over, Rose felt like the sun was shining full strength in a blaze of glory in her heart.

"I'm fine, Lachlan. I don't think I've ever been so fine."

Lachlan's face looked so perplexed Rose giggled.

That night, Rose woke with a start.

Who's calling me in the middle of the night? There aren't any babies due.

She was the wagon train doula and had been called many times to assist at births. She was so thankful most of the babies lived.

Just in case someone was there who needed her, she went to the back of the wagon and looked out. It was a magnificent scene. The moon shone brilliantly—lighting up the land. She breathed in the perfume of the night air, took one last look at the twinkling stars, decided she must have been imagining things, and was about to climb back under her bearskin when she heard it again. This time it was unmistakable. Her name was being called with such love. Rose was bewildered. It was Lachlan's voice. He was obviously asleep, calling her in his dreams.

Try as she might, she couldn't explain this away. Why was this man calling her name? Rose tried to dismiss the feelings in her heart, but couldn't. She felt loved—wanted. She somehow knew if it was required, that man would die for her. She knew Lachlan loved her. Deeply. She knew she was treasured—cherished.

This kind, gentle man loves me?

Rose fell asleep praying.

Dear Lord Jesus, is this why You placed the desire in my heart to go West. Was I supposed to meet Lachlan? I don't understand my feelings for him. What are your plans for us? Please show me clearly.

Sunday, September 1o, 1854

Dear Ma,
I have no idea if you will ever get this letter, but I'm compelled to write to you. I have a feeling you will expect what I'm about to say. You probably saw it in my messages long before I did. Lachlan is in love with me. Isn't that crazy? Don't ask me what I feel. I've never felt so confused in all my life. That's all I have to say about that.

We have a problem here. Guides often had the directions for a route in their heads. I've already told you our guide died just before we got to the Rocky Mountains, so we have no idea how to get to Oregon. Captain Whittaker died in a day—that's how fast cholera kills a man—so he had no time to explain the route to anyone else.

Some of the settlers decided they knew the best way to go, they were the majority, so we decided to stick together and follow them. Now we are hopelessly lost and in danger of running out of provisions. The trail we were on has ended at the side of a mountain.

When we left Independence, the trail boss said it was critical for us to leave in April if we hoped to reach Oregon before the snow.

We were told there could be snowstorms and severe cold weather in the mountains. The cold could lead to frostbite and death by freezing. We weren't worried. We would be safely out of the Rockies before the snow. He forgot to tell us sometimes the snow arrives early. It's only August. It's snowing.

So, now I must confess my hope to reach Oregon is dwindling. I don't know if you will ever see these letters while I am alive. I'm writing in the hopes that even if I die here in the mountains, someone, one day, will find the letters and send them to you.

The prospect of death is scary—and yet at the same time I am at peace—because I know where I am going. I know when my eyes close on Earth I will be standing in eternity with my Lord and Savior. We will meet in that beautiful place.

I love you, Ma.

Chapter Eighteen

Snow fell heavily through the night. This was so unexpected. The pioneers thought they had until September before the weather turned. Rose was thankful she had the bison hide. It provided extra warmth from the cold. It was the blanket Lachlan put on the ground for his bed. He insisted she have it.

Refusing to ride in the wagon, Rose wanted it to be as light as possible for the animals, but now her feet felt like they were nearly frozen. She was so tired as she warmed up by the fire. Rose glanced at Lachlan. He had such a kind face. He saw her looking at him, so he flashed her one of his dazzling smiles. Rose suddenly felt warm all over.

"Rose, would you like some tea?"

"That would be lovely. Thank you."

As Lachlan handed her the steaming cup, she couldn't help but notice his eyes. They looked so kind, so loving. His eyes even smiled at her. She had to look away or her own eyes would have betrayed her thoughts.

As they sat by the fire, Rose noticed the stars sparkled with a special brilliance in the inky, black sky. What was it about the cold that made the stars look even brighter? Peace filled Rose's heart, a peace past all understanding.

I don't want this night to end. This will be one of our last nights on the trail. I will soon have to say goodbye to this beautiful man. Why do I have such mixed feelings about that? I want to teach school, but...

"Rose, may I get the bison cover for you? You look cold."

"Thank you, Lachlan."

As he gently draped the robe over her shoulders, Rose was startled by his question.

"Rose, what are you thinking?"

Rose turned and gazed into his eyes. She couldn't possibly tell him what she had just been thinking.

She smiled and said, "Nothing much."

"It looks like we could have a storm tonight," Lachlan said as he scanned the darkening sky. There was the faintest light still on the horizon, but it was being covered by masses of churning, dark clouds. "We may have more snow. Would you like my bear skin tonight?"

Rose nearly cried. How could this man be so thoughtful?

"Lachlan James Smith, you're offering me your only cover? You'd freeze."

"Rose, I was so worried when I almost lost you. I would gladly give you my shirt too if it would keep you warmer."

"Thank you, Lachlan, but you need your blanket. I don't want you to freeze. Who would be so appreciative of my burnt biscuits?"

Lachlan didn't look up. He picked up the spoon he was whittling and started working on it. That was a good thing, because he would have been sad to see Rose crying. She was so overcome by the goodness of this man.

Lachlan didn't dare look at Rose. It was getting harder to hide his thoughts and feelings about this precious woman.

Looking across the fire at the kindest man she had ever met, Rose knew he meant every word he said. The man was the picture of integrity and honesty. He spoke only truth. He would give her his shirt and freeze if necessary so she would be warm. She knew he would give his life to save hers. She thought what a fine husband he would make for someone one day.

Tuesday, September 12, 1854

Dear Ma,
Lachlan said it was the fur traders who first opened this pass through the Rocky Mountains. They must have had a wild time carrying canoes and axes to clear a path. The rivers

we've seen have been crazy wild, so it's a wonder any of them lived to leave us journals about their trip.

We're thankful the people who came before us cleared the way so it's fairly easy to follow the route—except where there's snow. The mountain goats cling to the cliffs above us, following our progress with their enormous black eyes. I wonder how many wagon trains they've watched over the years?

We followed the Platte River through what was called the South Pass in Wyoming. As we traveled northwest, someone remembered Captain Whittaker saying we had to follow the Columbia River once we got to the Rockies.

Wednesday, September 13, 1854

Dear Ma,
The wagon trail has been treacherous. We had been following wagon tracks for days, on a fairly well-worn path, but now the ground is uneven and covered in snow. Boulders litter the path. The wagons lurch and groan. We wondered if we got off the path somehow. Some of the men went ahead to scout out the trail. They said we're in the right place, but we're stopped by a recent rock slide. Thankfully the men were able to clear the route in a day.

We have others issues besides the rock slide. There was no grassland for the animals. Provisions are getting low. Most folks are not prepared for snow. It's so cold, Ma. I'm writing this while sitting by the fire under a huge bearskin. My fingers are numb, but I'm determined to write you.

I love you, Ma.

The next morning, twenty-four men gathered to discuss what to do.
"Our lives are in grave danger."
"Bad choice of words."

"The animals can't continue without food."

"Well, there's no turning back now."

"If we push on, we should be at the end of the trail in about a month."

"That's a pretty big if."

"Well, if we don't, we're dead."

"Don't tell the women folk."

"What'll we do?"

"Gentlemen, unless God intervenes, we are dead."

"The game will be scarce in the mountains."

"We aren't prepared for snow."

"Men, we need a miracle. Now."

The men prayed, acknowledging their helplessness and need of God.

After they prayed, someone came up with an idea. They talked of abandoning a few wagons and having people share wagons for extra warmth. Chances of survival would be greater.

Some of the oxen could be used for food, and some could be tied behind to be used to replace the tired oxen pulling the wagons. The oxen getting too tired to go on would be eaten. Wagons not needed could be used for firewood. All agreed this was the wisest idea. It would be easier to find food for less animals.

That night the camp feasted on the first oxen around a roaring fire. Owen, Willow, and baby Seth moved in with Rose. Their wagon provided the wood for a roaring fire. It was far too cold for Lachlan to continue sleeping outdoors. He could easily get hypothermia and die. He now sleeps on the wagon floor. Rose insisted he have the bison hide back. The wagon was so much warmer with more bodies in it.

Friday, September 15, 1854

Dear Ma,
My fingers are numb as I write. I've never felt so cold. We traveled the entire day up a steep mountainside with fresh fallen snow. This was no small feat for the oxen pulling the wagons. Everyone walked or rode a horse, to lighten the load for the oxen. It was a miracle we made as much progress as we did. The mountains seemed to open up and by noon they were at our backs.

Tuesday, September 19, 1854

It will be fairly easy traveling now. There's no snow on the West side of the Rocky Mountains. The air is much warmer, and there seems to be a soft humidity. Must be because we are closer to the Pacific Ocean. It's still around six hundred miles to Oregon City, so we still have a month on the trail. After what we have experienced, it seems like we are on a Sunday picnic.

Ma, I'm missing Lachlan already, and we haven't even parted. I am cherishing my time with him, knowing our days together are numbered. Owen and Willow will be looking for a homestead near him. I'm glad he won't be completely by himself. I'm not sure how he will break land, plant crops, put up fences, raise animals, harvest, feed and clean up after the animals, make his own meals and wash his own clothes. I'm hoping he may still need a cook...haha.
I love you, Ma.

Saturday, September 23, 1854

Lachlan gently moved a wisp of Rose's hair off her face. This was their last night together. He had talked to God earlier in the day about his predicament.
"Dear Lord, You see my heart. You know I love Rose. There are no secrets with You. She is the kindest, gentlest, most loving

person I've ever met. I can't lose her. How can I say goodbye? I can't imagine my life without that woman. What do I do, Lord?"

After he prayed, Lachlan had the distinct feeling he should talk to Owen for advice.

"Owen, do you think asking Rose to live on a ranch in the country would be too much of a sacrifice for this city girl? She's already endured so much. She's probably looking forward to civilization."

"Well, you could ask her and let her make up her own mind," Owen said.

"But, is it fair to ask her to give up her dream of teaching? That's her reason to come to Oregon. It doesn't seem fair to ask her. Living on a ranch in the country isn't her dream."

"Well, you could ask her."

"The end of the trail will be upon us tomorrow. Do you think she would want to give up her dreams for me?"

"Just ask her."

"It's just that I've never met anyone like her. She makes me laugh, she says and does such unexpected things. She's so courageous, Owen. If the captain had let her come by herself, she would have."

"Yup, she's a pretty amazing girl. She saved my Willow's life. I'm much obliged to her."

"I'm so thankful she accepted my invitation to join me on this adventure. Asking her to be my cook just gave her a legitimate reason to come along."

"I'd say God had His hand in this whole thing."

Lachlan barely heard a word Owen said.

"It's her eyes. Have you noticed how they sparkle? They are sometimes so full of mischief."

"She's pretty special, all right."

"Do you think she'd want to marry a rancher? She's such a fine lady."

"You could always ask her, Lachlan."

"But I don't have much to offer her. She is a lot richer than I am."

"Do you really think wealth is important to Rose?"

"Well, no."

"Then just ask the girl to marry you and see what she says."

This was Lachlan's last chance to tell Rose how he felt before they were to go separate ways. He didn't know if that would be possible as something seemed to be stuck in his throat. Rose sat quietly watching the fire. The stars seemed to hold their breath, as Lachlan's face asked the question, "Can I really tell this woman how I feel about her?" He reached out and moved another stray wisp of hair off Rose's face. Rose smiled up at him. Her eyes sparkled like the stars.

"Rose, do you recall when we were back at Independence Rock? I went for a stroll to the rock by myself. You stayed back to make dinner."

"Yes. I remember."

"Well, I wanted to go by myself."

"Why?"

"I wanted to carve your name in the rock, right beside mine. I felt like it belonged there."

"Why didn't you show me?"

"I didn't want to scare you, Rose."

"What do you mean?"

"I wrote Lachlan & Rose Smith."

"What? You wrote that? Was that what Owen was hinting about at the campfire?"

"Yes."

There was a very awkward silence.

Lachlan suddenly felt very guilty. "I'm sorry, Rose. I had no right to write that."

"Nonsense, I think it's beautiful."

"You do?"

"Of course, Lachlan James Smith. I think you are the finest man I have ever met, so I feel honored you wrote that."

"Do you mean that, Rose?"

"Of course I do. You have been around me for over six months. You should know by now I only speak truth."

"Rose Caroline Murphy. I love you."

"I love you too."

"You do?"

"Heavens, yes. I've loved you for months!"

"You have?"

"Well, Rose, I beat you on that one. I've loved you since I first saw you sitting on that steamer trunk crying. I had the strongest impulse to grab you off that trunk and hold you and protect you and tell you everything was going to be alright. But, of course I couldn't. You never would have agreed to come with me as my cook."

"You're right."

"Well, tomorrow I guess you're planning to go into town to look for a place to teach?"

"Not necessarily."

"What do you mean?"

"Well, you mentioned something back in Independence about starving if you didn't have a cook."

"That's true, but I can make tea."

They both laughed at that, as just over six months before, that was all Rose could make.

"Rose Caroline Murphy, would you like to be Rose Caroline Smith?"

"Well, Lachlan James Smith, how can I say no. It's already written in stone."

Lachlan scooped Rose up in his arms and held her. He murmured in her ear, "Rose, I will love, protect, cherish, and hug you all the days God gives me."

"Lachlan, I will respect and honor you all the days God gives me."

He kissed the top of her head and they both cried tears of joy.

"God, thank You for this beautiful, precious woman."

"Lord God, thank You for this beautiful, amazing man."

Sunday, September 24, 1854

Dear Ma,
I have a feeling you already suspect what I'm about to tell you. Lachlan has asked me to be Mrs. Rose Caroline Smith, and I have accepted his proposal. I can imagine you and the girls laughing and dancing at that news. I dearly love the man.

How could I say anything but yes? He is honestly the kindest, and most thoughtful, loving, and godly man I have ever met. I wish you and the girls could come to the wedding. I am sure it's going to be special. I'm going to wear the beautiful white lace dress I bought in New York. The one you embroidered.

Willow and my friend Jane have kindly said they would be my bridesmaids…or is it bride's matrons because they are both married? Both are with child, so I will actually have four people with me. Both ladies have lavender-colored dresses. Oh, I forgot to mention. The wedding is in one day. We have to have it soon or all our wedding guests will be gone.

Our friends put some money together for a wedding gift. We told them we didn't want any gifts, they need their money to buy their land and seeds and to build their homes—but they insisted. They want us to spend a few nights for a honeymoon at a hotel in Oregon City. How sweet of them to do this for us! We don't need their money, but we know they did this with love so we had to accept.

This time on the Oregon Trail has been the deadliest, most treacherous adventure I've ever embarked on. Even so, I wouldn't trade a minute of it for anything. The scenery has been breathtaking, seeing the vast herds of buffalo with their huge dust clouds has been amazing, putting up with mosquitos, dust, and mud has built character, watching the spectacular sunrises and sunsets has been awesome, and seeing the vast starry skies has been humbling. I can see why King David once glanced at the sky and asked, "Who is man, Lord, that you even consider him?"

Learning to cook has been fun, and the friendships I have formed will go into eternity. I have discovered when I submit to God, and ask Him to lead and be in charge, amazing things happen.

I'll write you when we have settled, and then send this epistle with the next person heading East.

I love you and miss you, Ma.

EPILOGUE

It was the end of the trail. Folks were about to part company, each headed to different destinations. Lachlan blasted the trumpet for old time's sake – it sounded as terrible as ever – and made an announcement. People gathered, wondering what the noise was all about.

"Friends, it is with great joy I announce Rose Caroline Murphy has agreed to be my wife. I'd be mighty obliged if you'd stay just for another few days to help us celebrate."

Cheers rang out. There were a lot of knowing looks and I told you so's. Not a soul left for their new homes. No one wanted to miss the fun. The best feast and party of the entire trip was Lachlan and Rose's wedding. Of course, Rose looked radiant in her white lace gown. Jane and Willow were beautiful bridesmaids. There was such joy and rejoicing.

Monday, September 21, 1857

Dear Ma,

We purchased a large tract of land a few miles out of Oregon City. Willow and Owen live on the next homestead. There's water from the Clackamas River for the cattle. There are rolling hills, lakes and beautiful forests. It is lovely here. The men worked together to build our houses. Log houses are so beautiful. I even have real windows. The men clear the land, raise cattle and crops together. It's so beautiful. I'm so happy.

I taught grades one to twelve for two years, just outside of Oregon City in a one-room schoolhouse. Every morning Lachlan hitched a wagon, drove me to the schoolhouse, and then picked me up after school. On cold days he always had bear skins to wrap me up in. His kindness has never stopped. He is such a good man. Teaching ended for me when baby William was born on August 12th, 1857, on his Uncle Owen William's birthday.

I love you, Ma.

Rose sent the letter with someone heading east. She had no idea if she would ever hear from Ma in this lifetime. One day, Hank at the General Store smiled and handed her an envelope.

Monday, September 21, 1857
Dear Rose,
I just received all your letters. I am so glad to hear from you. The fact that I didn't hear from you for years was stressful. I'm not sure why there was such a long delay in getting them. Maybe they were at the bottom of someone's saddle bag? Congratulations on your wedding and all your exciting news!

My, it was fascinating hearing of your adventures. I must say I laughed and cried often while reading of the joys and dangers along the trail. I'm glad you dated the letters. I was able to check back what I wrote in my diary on those dates. The night before you nearly drowned, God had me praying all night for you. I could not sleep. I begged him to let you live. I am so thankful He answered my prayers.

The dates you had scarlet fever were rough days for me. I wrote in my diary that I could not get you out of my mind. God had me fasting and praying for your safety. So many have died from scarlet fever. What a miracle of God's grace you lived. I ran into a young woman who was on the wagon train with you. Her name's Amanda. She asked me to tell you someone came along and helped her get back to Independence. They are married now.

I'm glad there is a pony express now. I'm sure you'll get this letter. It's amazing letters only take ten days instead of sometimes years to travel from coast to coast.

I am thrilled you had the opportunity to teach school—and I am so excited at how God is leading you. I am thankful you have a godly husband who loves you dearly. From the way you described him at the very start of the Oregon Trail, I could tell he was a very special man. I wondered if God had brought you two together. The circumstances had His fingerprints all over them. I pray God continues to bless you and keep you, my child. I look forward to meeting you and your precious family in Heaven one day.

I am still looking after all the young women God sends my way, but I must tell you, I have never had such a lovely house guest as Rose Caroline Murphy. You were much more than a guest. You were the daughter I never had.

Much Love,
Ma Morgan

Between Lachlan and Owen's families, fourteen children grew up together. They were all greatly loved, and both families had plenty of puppies and swings.

And now, please enjoy the first chapter of the next Prairie Rose Collection story, Aria by Shonda Czeschin Fischer.

Chapter One of ARIA by SHONDA FISCHER

Spring of 1865 Independence, Missouri

"I can't believe we are finally here." Aria Cane nibbled at the cracker before taking a sip of hot tea to wash it down. Swallowing hard, she tried to force the rolling of her stomach into submission. A cold sweat broke across her drawn up face, her tightly closed eyes slowly opened as nausea passed "Aria, dear, are you okay? You seem a little peaked."

"Uncle John's warm hand rested along her cheek.

"I'm fine or at least I will be the sooner we get away from Missouri."

Aria gazed upon the wagon trains camped, waiting to pull out, women hurried about fixing their families a bit of breakfast excited to start their journey.

Cool morning air stirred the wisp of hair that already broke free from her braid tickling her neck while smoke from the campfires cause her stomach to roll from the strong smell. The clomping of horse hooves drew Aria from her thoughts, she looked over her shoulder as an older man approached them.

Wagon master Hank Finch sat tall in his saddle making his way from wagon to wagon.

"Morning Cane family. We'll be pulling out in thirty minutes. Bank your fire and be ready to roll we must stay on schedule."

Uncle John stood with a coffee cup in hand. His blue eyes sparkled at the excitement of the new adventure. "Yes, sir, Mr. Finch, we'll be ready." He said pouring the last of his coffee over the fire, sending a plumb of smoke into the air with a woosh.

Aria drug her tired frame from the log her backside occupied and began cleaning up the morning meal. Cousin Trevor who at seventeen was tall and stout for his age, help hitch the mules to the wagon. Pouring the last of the coffee from the pot onto the fire, she kicked dirt from the ground making sure all embers were extinguished.

Pulling a shawl around her shoulders, Aria immersed the tin plates in the warm water inside the small bucket. She quickly wiped them off and placed them back in the storage box attached to the side of the wagon. With a sigh, she trudged back to the fire pit and upended the water onto the ground, careful not to step on the little purple flowers that were blooming along the path.

The blue sky stretched out before her as the warble of a blue jay sang its serenade. Aria's lips turned down at the corners, she stared out over the vast prairie with trepidation.

Uncle John rested his hand on her shoulder.

"Will you be walking, or do you want to ride with me?"

Aria shoulders sagged at the thought of doing either. "I think I'll walk for now."

With a squeeze to her shoulder, he drew her against his side placing a kiss on her forehead.

"Don't overexert yourself, rest when you need it. You hear me?"

With a nod, she blinked back the moisture pooling in her eyes.

Mr. Finch's voice carried down the wagons as he shouted, "Wagon ho!"

The first of the wagons began rolling forward. Uncle John glanced back over Independence one last time before climbing up into the wagon to leave behind the only life that they had known.

The prairie grass waved about for miles upon endless miles as she trudged along the wagon. Aria pulled her bonnet up over her head tying the strings beneath her chin, squinting against the bright sun. This would be her life for the next six months. It was all because of her that Uncle John had to sell everything and head west.

When the fever came through their small town and took her parents and Aunt Olivia, Uncle John moved her in with him and cousin Trevor. Aria's father younger than John by two years, had told her stories of their days as young boys. The brothers made a pact that when they grew up and had families of their own that they would share land, never to live far from one another.

They kept that promise and bought enough acreage they could raise their families on and be neighbors. Aria loved Uncle John as she did her own father and knew he loved her like a daughter. A tear trickled down her cheek leaving a trail through the dust that settled on her face. Why did she have to make such a stupid mistake that would take them from the home that held so many memories.

The train moved slow and steady all morning, the wheels and animals leaving a trail of flat prairie grass behind. Aria pressed a hand into the small of her back, trudging forward on legs shaky with fatigue glad that the wagons had stopped. When a very unladylike rumble erupted from her stomach she sighed and began throwing together some biscuits and bacon left from the morning meal when a curly-headed toddler raced to her, squealing.

"Ida Mae, where are you?" A young girl about the same age as Aria with golden blonde hair and blue eyes called out after the tiny being.

Ida Mae's tiny hand grasped a fistful of Aria's skirts and buried her pudgy little face in them with a giggle. With coffeepot in hand

Aria stumbled trying to keep from falling as the little waif threw her off balance.

"I'm so sorry." The young girl's cheeks pinked up reaching for Ida Mae. "Ida Mae got away from me and took off thinking me chasing her was a game."

Aria's eyes twinkled as the little child clapped her hands at being swung up on the hip of the more grown-up version of herself.

"No harm done, she just surprised me is all."

"Where are my manners? I'm Mary Lloyd, and this is my little sister Ida Mae." Mary bounced the little girl on her hip, eliciting another giggle from the child.

"Nice to meet you Mary, my name is Aria Cane." She said, leaning in and tickling Ida Mae under her chin.

The little girl tucked her head against her shoulder with a giggle trying to keep from being tickled again.

"We are in the wagon behind yours, and I guess my little sister likes you. She doesn't usually take to strangers."

Mary shifted Ida Mae on her hip to get a better hold on her.

Aria swatted at a fly that buzzed around her with a grimace on her face.

"She sure is cute, how is she doing with the journey so far?"

Mary sighed, "Well, she wants to get down and walk, so I try to help ma by letting her walk with me some, but Ida Mae can be a handful."

Mary brushed the child's blonde curls out of her eyes before placing a kiss on her temple.

Aria placed the coffeepot on the tiny fold-down table on the side of the wagon.

"I'd be happy to walk with you, maybe with the two of us, we can keep her corralled."

"Are you sure? That would be wonderful, I would enjoy getting to know you better." Mary said, observing her fussy little sister rubbing her eyes with puckered lips.

"I'll let you get Ida Mae back to the wagon, she looks tired. But I'll come to your wagon before we take off so we can walk together. Aria rubbed the small child's back, who now rested her head against Mary's chest.

Mary headed back to her wagon with a skip in her step, Aria's smile spread across her face at the aspect of making a new friend. Trevor and Uncle John finished unhitching the mules to graze and walked toward her. Aria quickly unwrapped the biscuits and strips of bacon, laying them on a plate.

Pouring lukewarm coffee into tin mugs, she handed the men their coffee and gave each a biscuit and bacon sandwich. At the rumble of her stomach, she took the last biscuit and coffee and sat crossed legged on the ground. Tall prairie grass danced all around them like a sea of green pulsing with a heartbeat of its own mesmerizing her into a stare.

Aria sat her cup to the side and laid back with arms folded behind her head, staring up into the bright blue sky. Peace flowed over her as a yawn escaped. Letting watery eyes fluttered shut for what seemed like only a few heartbeats when a firm hand shook her shoulder.

"Aria, get up, it's time to head out again." Trevor squatted next to her with his long hair falling across his eyes.

Sitting up, Aria caught sight of others hitching up their mules or horses to wagons. Rubbing at her eyes with a slender hand she stood, and wiped at her skirts to rid remnants of grass that clung to her.

"Trevor, let Uncle John know that I'm going to walk with my new friend Mary. Her family is the wagon behind ours." Stooping, she picked up the tin mug on the ground, placing it and the others back in a small bucket to wash when they stopped for the evening.

Aria hurried her steps to Mary's wagon, where a tall boy about the age of sixteen with a face full of blemishes and blonde hair helped to hitch the team to the wagon. Mary held Ida Mae out to an older woman who must be her mother before greeting Aria.

The wagon master called out, and the wagons lurched forward right when Aria reached Mary's side.

"That sure was a short rest." Aria yawned, tucking wayward pieces of hair back into her bonnet.

Mary eyed the prairie before them as she slowed her steps to keep from pulling Ida Mae along.

"I barely had time to write in my journal once I got Ida Mae laid down. I want to write a little each day about our journey, so someday my children will read what we did."

"Do you have a beau?" Aria studied Mary with raised eyebrows.

Mary's eyes lit up at the question. "No, but I plan on finding me one on the trail."

Aria's eyes softened with a smile at the enthusiasm in Mary's voice.

"Do you have a fellow in mind?"

"I've seen a couple of handsome boys that I wouldn't mind getting to know." Mary giggled, batting her eyelashes.

Aria shook her head with a sigh.

"I had a beau, but I wasn't what his parents wanted in a wife. His parents were from old money and wanted him to marry another girl from a prominent family in the area. They threatened to disinherit him if he married me. I guess he loved money more than me because here I am without him." Aria said with a shrug of her shoulders.

Mary tripped over a rock, grabbing Aria's arm to keep herself upright.

"I'm so sorry you had to go through that. I would rather be poor than treat another person that way, you're better off without him."

Aria blinked back the moisture that sprang to her eyes as she reached out and plucked a piece of tall grass from the prairie. "Yeah, I guess you're right."

"Who knows, maybe you will find someone you're interested in on the wagon train?" Mary bumped Aria with a shoulder and a cheeky smile.

Aria couldn't entertain that thought. She had a secret to keep, and a beau would only make things worse for her and her family. She needed to focus on getting to Oregon and forging a new life and nothing else. Keep perfect pace with Mary as they tromped along beside the rolling wagons, Aria wiped the sweat from her brow.

"I'd rather wait until I get to Oregon, it's too soon for me. Besides, what if we liked the same boy?"

Mary's eyebrows shot up.

"I never thought about that. One of us would have a broken heart, and it could even destroy our friendship. Promise me that won't happen."

Mary pulled at the neck of the dress, trying to cool herself down with a wave of a hand.

Aria lifted her face to the subtle breeze.

"I promise that won't happen because I'm not interested in finding a beau, at least not on this trip."

Walking in silence, Aria let her thoughts wander with the clomping of the mules and the squeaking of the wagon wheels. She yearned to share her secret with her new friend but that wasn't possible, she must keep it to herself. Aria prayed God would forgive her for what she'd done and give her the strength to get through this trip so she could start a new life.

4th annual Prairie Roses Collection, 23 covered wagon stories!

All the 2022 Prairie Roses Collection Stories:

ELLA   Book 12 by Nancy Fraser
Can a widow with children find a second chance at happiness in a new home?

CALLI   Book 13 by Donna Schlachter
A newborn needs a mother, but can Calli uproot her life to care for the infant, going back east with a train of disgruntled pioneers?

LANEY   Book 14 by Vickie McDonough
A young woman fleeing her past runs head long into her future on the Santa Fe Trail.

SABRA   Book 15 by Patricia PACJAC Carroll
A wild journey and ornery camel throw opposites together, but can they stick?

PEARL Book 16 by Zina Abbott
Men go to mountaintops to pray. Women, caring for hearth and home, stay too busy to climb, so God comes to her.

GLORY Book 17 by Marisa Masterson
Dead set on making Pike's Peak and its goldfields, Glory's father leave her little choice but to go. Will they make it, leaving so late in the season?

ROSE Book 18 by Rena Groot
Will Rose depend on God to help her complete her journey west?

ARIA Book 19 by Shonda Fischer
Forgiving the past changes the future.

ELSIE Book 20 by KC Hart
Their futures are all planned, but neither consider God has a more perfect one.

AMITY Book 21 by Linda Carroll-Bradd
Will a hasty decision bring disaster, or will the journey forge bonds neither Amity nor Shawe imagined?

AMY Book 22 by Angela Lain
A callous father considers selling his daughter. Who can save her?

JO Book 23 by Caryl McAdoo
Not a good time to fall in love, but God . . . Who will she choose?

Previous Prairie Roses Collections

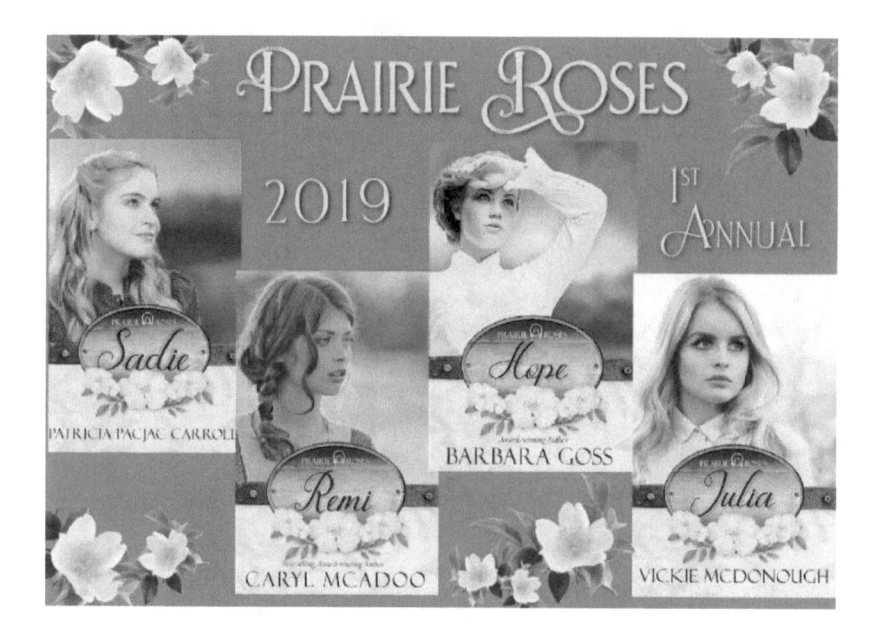

All the Prairie Roses authors hope you will enjoy all the stories of our collection and that you'll bless them with a quick review—posted around (Amazon, GoodReads, BookBub, Facebook, your blog!—while the story is still fresh on your mind. No need for a long, drawn-out synopsis; just a few of your own words why you liked it. Maybe mention a favorite character or scene. Make it easy on yourself!

THANK YOU SO MUCH ahead of time!

Prairie Roses Collection One: - 2019

SADIE by Patricia PACJAC Carroll	book one
REMI by Caryl McAdoo	book two
HOPE by Barbara Goss	book three
JULIA by Vickie McDonough	book four

Prairie Roses Collection Two - 2020

LILAH by Caryl McAdoo	book five
SUSAN by Patricia PACJAC Carroll	book six
KATE by Donna Schlachter	book seven

Prairie Roses Collection Three - 2021

RUTH by Caryl McAdoo	book eight
TESS by Annee Jones	book nine
SOPHIE by Patricia PACJAC Carroll	book ten
CADI by Linda Carroll-Bradd	book eleven

Prairie Roses Collection Four – 2022

ELLA by Nancy Fraser	book twelve
CALLI by Donne Schlachter	book thirteen
LANEY by Vickie McDonough	book fourteen
SABRA by Patricia PACJAC Carroll	book fifteen
PEARL by Zina Abbott	book sixteen

GLORY by Marisa Masterson   book seventeen

ROSE by Rena Groot   book eighteen

ARIA by Shonda Fischer   book nineteen

ELSIE by KC Hart   book twenty

AMITY by Linda Carroll-Bradd   book twenty-one

AMY by Angela Lain   book twenty-two

JO by Caryl McAdoo   book twenty-three

Acknowledgements

I fully realize everything we have is a gift from God.
We can do nothing, and we have nothing, apart from Him.
Thank You, Lord, for being so amazing and giving me a love
(okay, an addiction) for writing.

Thank you Caryl McAdoo for inviting me to be part of this
beautiful collection with so many gifted authors. Thank you for
patiently helping me learn how to be a writer in a book
collection.

Thank you to my editors and formatters, Fixer Fairy,
Lia McGunigle, and Debbey Cozonne,
for all your work in making Rose look beautiful.

Thank you Randi Gammons for the gorgeous cover design.

Thank you to all who inspired me as I wrote this book.
Most of Rose's "friends" are real people.
Thank you Cindy, Stephanie, Kim, Marcia, Crystal, Wendy,
Debbey, Phyllis, German Oma, Betty, Connie, Rory, Renee,
Kathy, and Cindi. I appreciate all your
inspiring comments about life and marriage.

Thank you, Timberly, for the great near drowning scene idea.

Thank you, dear Reader, for reading my novel.
You have only a certain numbers of hours in this life,
and you shared some of them with me. I am honored.
I have a special message for you on the next page.

Author's Note

Dear Reader,

I'm so grateful you've read my novel. I hope you found it gave God glory and spoke to your heart about His great love. There are a few special things I'd like you to know about Rose.

~ I prayed for inspiration for the photo for my cover. The cover photo is my university graduation photo. (It was God's idea. Honest.)

~ The dates on Ma's letters are actual dates. For example, Tuesday, September 12, 1854 really was a Tuesday.

~ I named this book after my grandmother, Rose. As far as I know, I never met my father's mother, Rose. Her life, and my dad's, were an enigma to me. While writing this book I found out Rose had two other grandchildren I knew nothing about—my brother and sister I didn't know existed. God is so amazing!

Reviews are so important to authors, so would you please take the time to leave a quick review at Amazon, Goodreads, your blog, and anywhere you enjoy reading about books. Of course, tell your friends. Stop by my Facebook page. I love connecting! The links are on the next page.

I pray that God will bless you, that His loving kindness and favor will envelop you!

Love & blessings,

Rena Groot

All Rena's Titles

A Life Set Free

A True Story About the Love and Faithfulness of God

"…a moving testimony of the liberating power of the love of Jesus to bring healing to broken lives. This story will encourage readers that nothing is impossible with God when we are fully surrendered to His loving care — that He will transform every tear and sorrow to bring forth a life streaming with beauty, compassion, and abundant fruitfulness."

Karen Davis,
Worship Director/Co-Founder Carmel Congregation, Haifa, Israel

The Narrow Path Trilogy

(Meme by Caryl McAdoo)

The Narrow Path Trilogy takes you on a journey that began before the dawn of time when angels rebelled and the dark, broken days of Earth began. Through the imagery of the seals and the trumpets of Revelation, God has revealed the terrible reality of the Antichrist's reign and the wrath to come.

"The future of the world, your future, my future is spelled out in living technicolor (in the narrow Path Trilogy). The question is, how soon will that future become reality today? More importantly, are you ready for eternity and have you already chosen where you will spend it?"

Steve Krumlauf,

Signature voice of Jan Markell's Understanding the Times

Manhunt
Only the Strong Survive

Now is the time of the end. The terrifying reality is Josh is being pursued by the Manhunters. His family has been captured. Are they alive? To survive the Tribulation, the reign of terror of the king, the children's prison, the re-education camp, PTSD, addictions, the great deception, and betrayal by family and friends, deep faith in God and extreme courage are required. Only the strong survive. The ancient narrow path is calling. Come.

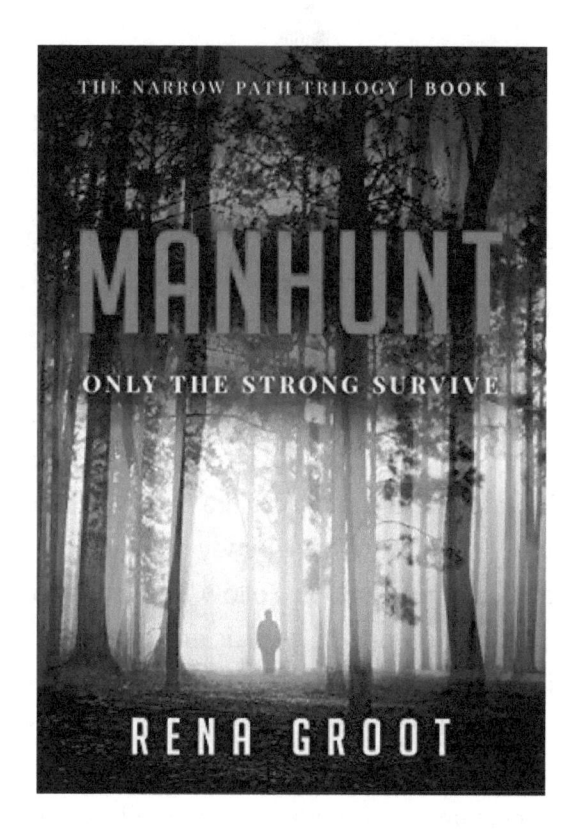

Transhuman
Will We Obey God or Play God?

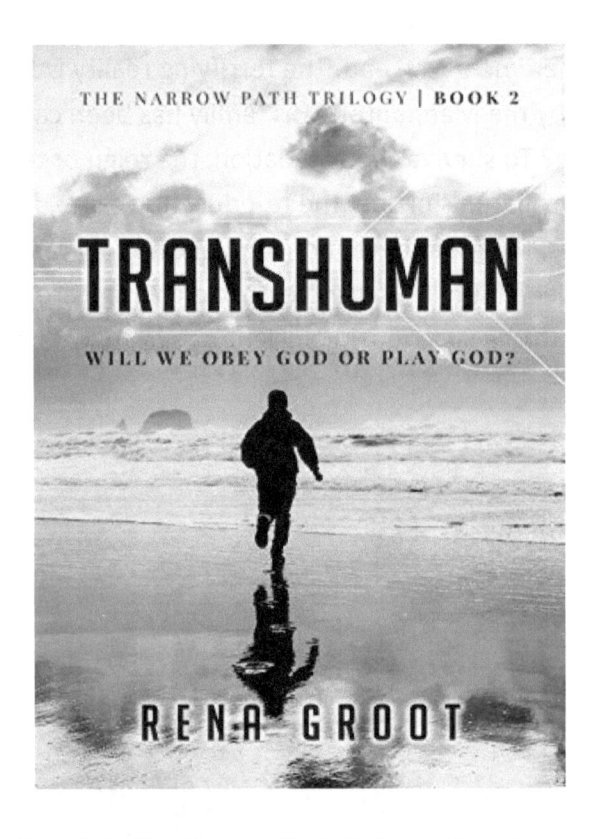

The second book in the Narrow Path Trilogy, Transhuman is based on what the world could look like at the halfway point in the Tribulation. The Rapture has already taken place. The chaos that ensues is horrendous. Follow Josh as he comes up against an apocalyptic world of genetic engineering, transhumanism, artificial intelligence, child-sex trafficking, super soldiers, and deception in the church. The question Josh is asking is, "Will We Obey God or Play God?" Soon time will be no more. The curtains are opening on the world stage. Come.

Convergence
A Window Into Eternity

Convergence leads us down a narrow path to an apocalyptic world that was foretold thousands of years ago. All the end-time puzzle pieces are aligning. The convergence—the merging of prophetic signs—is accelerating alarmingly."

The climactic showdown between good and evil is upon us. It is a time of horror. The seven thunders and the seven bowls of the wrath of God have been unleashed on Earth.

Beyond the nightmare, a time of beauty, peace, and love awaits. The curtain is being pulled back and you are invited into the drama. Come.

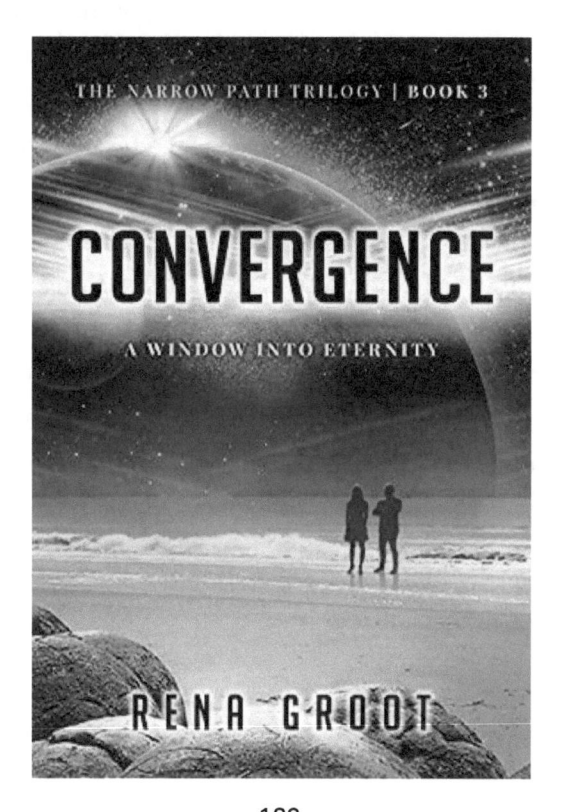

Broken to Beautiful
Transformed By God's Power Journal

What do you do when life sends trauma and pain where you hoped for love and respect?
Have you felt broken? Betrayed? Traumatized? Not enough? That was me. Life looked pretty sad. I had a choice. I could lay crying on the floor, or I could trust God and allow His words of love and peace to penetrate my heart.

I wisely chose to trust and discovered strength and courage far beyond my own. I also discovered godly, beautiful, transformational steps that have led me to greater health in every dimension ~ spirit, soul and body. I'd love to help you discover them too. This Journal can be used alone or as a valuable resource along with the course, Broken to Beautiful ~ Transformed by God's Power.

Mommy & Baby's Journal

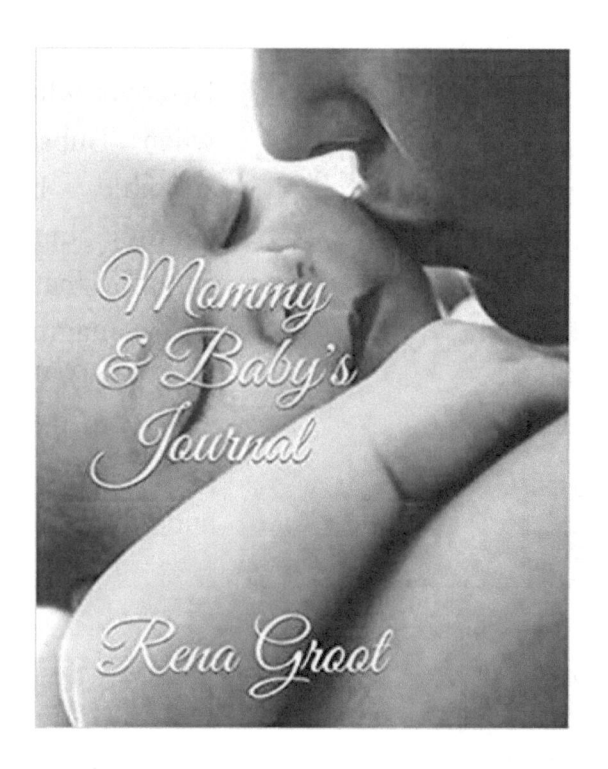

Dear Mommy,

This Journal is for you to write about your precious unborn baby and will give you information about your baby's monthly development. Or, this would be a precious gift for an expectant mom. People from all over the world have contributed comments and prayers for you and your unborn child. This will be a special keepsake of your thoughts and prayers for your baby while God formed them in the womb.

Bubs Bunny Goes to Camp

Discover what happens when Bubs, a very adorable but very neurotic bunny, goes to camp. What will his wild imagination tell him next? Will he be safe from the hippos, polar bears, alligators, and more?

About the Author

Ever since I walked into my first-grade classroom as a little awe-struck girl, I dreamed of being a school teacher. Dreams do come true. I earned a Bachelor of Education from the University of Alberta and a Masters of Religious Education from the Southern Baptist Seminary in Cochrane, Alberta.

I have been a teacher in Canada and China. I wrote A Life Set Free –a story about the faithfulness and love of God—while sitting under a mosquito net in China. That's when my addiction to writing was born.

God has given me the honor of being an ambassador with "The Department of Eternal Affairs" to so many cool places ~ I never dreamed I would one day be praying with a voodoo queen in Haiti, staying at an orphanage in Uganda, sharing the love of God in Mexico City as an earthquake shook the ground under my feet, leading a dying woman to Jesus in a hut in Belize ~ so many exciting stories.

>renagroot.com (blog)
>renagroot@yahoo.ca (email)
>https://amzn.to/376xOrv (Amazon)
>https://www.facebook.com/rena.groot
>https://rena-groot.mykajabi.com
>(Broken to Beautiful—Transformed by God's Power online course)

Made in United States
Troutdale, OR
04/16/2025